Lost Lovers
by Tom Richards

<u>About Lost Lovers</u>

Grace Upendo (32) is a Sexually-abused Black Swahili African. Despite her strength of character, she is haunted by a dark past. Full of fear, and unable to reach out to those who could help heal her scarred heart, she is saved by the man of her dreams, **Sean Hope**. But when Sean understands how damaged she is due to past horrors of rape and abuse, and despite his great love for her, he comes to realize that to heal her he must leave her.

Years later, when Grace finally gains the courage to escape from **Jester Jones**, an abusive Australian sailing yacht owner, she begins a frightening voyage of discovery through stormy seas to an uncharted, magical island only 150 nautical miles from Brisbane, Australia. There, in this unearthly land of honey, filled with lakes, streams, stunning golden beeches, mysterious creatures, dark forests and tall mountains, she begins to find new hope.

On the island an adventure begins with a magical play, LOST LOVERS (yes, the stage play name is the same as the novel, but you'll soon understand when you read it, and will find the play quite amusing and entertaining!), a raucous play based in part on Shakespeare's *A Midsummer Night's Dream*. Its cast of characters, all animals and insects and talking bees, too, even include a talking two-headed Kangaroo called Sue the Two-Headed Roo. But as the humans and animals begin rehearsals, Grace soon discovers she cannot understand its cast of misfit characters. Filled with confusion, she is taken into the depths of the sea, to Fish School, by a white-faced Common Dolphin. There, beneath the churning waves, she finally learns her lesson: she can talk to the magical animals and even the two-headed Roo. Having found the key, Grace is taken back to the magical island and dreams of a beach. Buried beneath it is a bright diamond engagement ring which Sean had tried to give her twice, years before, but which she had refused. And when she recognises the Roo as Sean, and he understands that Grace is his lost lover, then the magic ends and the reality of a loving future begins.

<u>**What Readers Say:**</u>

This is a story told mostly in iambic pentameter, much like the greatest playwright of our times, William Shakespeare, used so adroitly. A novella of magical realism, the story interweaves a tragic romance and a hysterical adventure played out on a wonderful, glorious Pacific Island. *Lost Lovers* is a story readers won't be able to put down.
***George Lambe**, UK*

…this is a fascinating mixture of several literary genres, and to me, that is one of its greatest   strengths.
***Barbara Klaw**, Chicago, Illinois, United States*

Think *Peter Pan* combined with William Shakespeare's funniest plays including *A Midsummer Night's Dream* and *Romeo + Juliet*. That's the novella that Tom Richards has woven together. My heart went out to the protagonist, Grace. She faces so many issues that many women of color in this world face today. But due to her strong character, and the loving loyalty of her partner, she prevails.
***Lauret Cusins**, Mobile, Alabama, United States*

A bull's eye! This was one of the best short novels I've read in a long time. I have no doubt it will win many awards and rightly so.
***Shauna O'Neill**, Sydney, Australia*

Because there are enough 'jam boy' references here to make Smuckers blush, then I get the story. Honestly, my recommendation for ye (and I mean it) is to put out the *Heartbreak & Happiness* Anthology and see what reaction there is to Ham-and-Eggs; if people love its Wit-and-Whimsy, then this new book is for them.
***Will Arnold** (occasional poet), my best friend from Chicago, Illinois, United States (fortunately, this book isn't dedicated to him because there's simply no room left on the dedication page!)*

Lost Lovers

Cover design: Toqueer Shahid. Find him at
https://www.fiverr.com/touqeershahid95?source=inbox.
Edited by: Grammargal. Find her at
https://www.fiverr.com/grammargal?source=inbox.
Illustrations provided by Sumit Kumar (SKG Animation). For all of
their many capabilities go to: www.skganimation.com

To contact the author, email tomrichards141@gmail.com.

Books by Tom Richards

<u>Fiction for Adults</u>

Dolphin Song

Always Come Home

Happiness & Heartbreak, *an Anthology*
(by Tom Richards and Various Authors)

The Dazzling Helen Fox,
a new adventure based on a true-life story
To be launched in Autumn 2022

<u>Fiction for Young Adults</u>

Hotfoot
Hotfoot 2: Lucky's Revenge
The Lost Scrolls of Newgrange
The Den Adventure (TV tie-in for Ireland's The Den Show)

<u>Non-Fiction</u>

A Survivors Guide to Living in Ireland, multiple editions

Lost Lovers is the author's third novel for the Adult Marketplace. As a sort of sequel to *Dolphin Song*, the best-selling romantic fantasy, it reads nothing like that story though, Dear Readers, you may recognize some of the characters. For more information visit www.tomrichards.ie.

DEDICATION

To my Aunt Wini Pethtel, the most loving and devout
Auntie in the world;

In Loving Memory of my great friend
US Army Lt Colonel Steven Courtney, A Brave Soldier;

To the Nurses, Doctors and Staff of Bantry General Hospital, who
cared for me as I recovered from my recent heart attack;

To Ron Raben, RIP, the author's High School English and Drama
Teacher, who taught me how to write and act in stage plays and
musicals;

To John Ficca, my theatre professor at Illinois Wesleyan University
who also taught me how to write, as well as the IWU Classes of
1977/1978 who acted in the stage play,
A Midsummer Night's Dream (what a wonderful memory!);

&

As ever, to my true-to-life inspiration: my partner,
My best friend, a brave soul who never complains about *anything*, and
my future wife (we've been
engaged for some time)

CARMEL MURRAY

Table of Contents

Part One: The Voyage Begins

<u>Chapter One</u>

My name is Kylie Whipple and even though I'm eighty-three and white-skinned, I'm the best friend of a Swahili dark-skinned young African woman who grew up like a Saint but soon got into trouble due to a love that was lost yet found again.

As the story moves on, sometimes, dear Reader, it will read in typical narrative fashion but at other times, when the novel travels to a mysterious Island which is much more than magical, it will read in Iambic Pentameter, just like the Great Bard and Playwright, William Shakespeare, used to write. It's more fun this way and much more compelling; a way of playing with your imagination that you'll soon find so entertaining.

So let me stop this brief prologue that's the beginning of *Lost Lovers*, and turn to Grace, the star of our story, and a woman you'll soon find both emotionally troubled but holy as a saint. So, hold onto your hats, and get ready for a story, and let's start by describing the problems that our Heroine faces at the beginning of this tale of happiness and heartbreak, where Grace is confronted with the horrors of a violent boyfriend on a yacht which has the same name as this novel. But take heart, all you readers, by the end of this tale happiness finally prevails when her lost lover Sean finds her again after so many years, and the couple are blessed in a Glory so Eternal it can hardly be real – but it is.

***

Grace Upendo (whose surname means 'love' in Swahili) was working on the sailing yacht Lost Lovers, getting it ready for the tourists who were soon expected to board. Dressed in an unbecoming Nautical Costume she was forced to wear by her employer, Jester Jones, a wanna be rich guy and a tyrant, Grace pulled out a fold-down table and graced it with a snow-white tablecloth, which contrasted beautifully with her ebony black skin. Next, she laid out a meal just for two: she first set the best of China and real silverware. Then she placed a main dish on the table of Prawns with Green Noodles topped with a lovely thick sauce. Next, she set down pudding cups capped with Fresh Red Strawberries piled high with whirls of Snowy White Whipped Cream which made it a perfect dessert. Finally, she placed on the table a golden bucket holding a bottle of chilled Champaign (Dom Perignon – these foreign tourists demanded the best from yacht owner Jester!) and beside it two crystal glasses (Waterford, the most famous crystal in Ireland, and the world!)

Finished. She spun from the table, inadvertently brushing the glasses with her elbow. They toppled from the surface and shattered on the wooden deck. As they did her boss, the yacht's Australian owner, dressed in a white captain's uniform complete with blue and gold chevron's on both shoulders, ran out from the Cabin where he'd been napping, letting Grace do all the work.

"Don't you know those were *real* crystal glasses and expensive, you fool!" Jester shouted at poor Grace. "I got them from a very rich customer in Dublin as a tip – I suspect you don't even know where Ireland is. Now snap to it and clean up that mess before the arrival of our guests!"

As he slunk off the deck, a middle-aged couple clambered aboard, both dressed in misfit outfits that Thurston Howell III and Eunice 'Lovely' Howell might wear in television's *Gilligan's Island* (the 1960's TV Series). They were a sight to behold! The male tourist, Huxley Bullak, was dressed like a fancy privileged Sailboat Commodore, complete with navy coat and a silly Commodore's double-pointed hat. His idiot wife, Carliss Bullak, wore a polka dot, knee-length dress, and floppy white hat, the best that Oxford Street could offer. (She thought she was stunning even though she was anything but).

Meanwhile, their two heavy travel trunks were carried aboard by African servants. The trunks brimmed with clothes for ten weeks, even though the scheduled voyage aboard the Lost Love was for only six days. The awkward luggage was over a tonne-weight each and the poor servant couple, an Aboriginal husband and his good wife, sweated desperately in the Australian morning sun, their neckerchiefs were soaked, don't you bet! The snooty tourists had heard the ruction over the broken crystal glasses and saw Grace's humiliation by the sweat on her brow and her shaking hands. Despite this, the Commodore ordered Grace:

"You! African Princess!" he mewled, thinking it was a complement but it was anything but, "Take my coat and my hat. Now pronto," he clapped.

As Grace strode to comply, Jester ordered Grace to cast-off the yacht. Caught between the two orders Grace didn't know what to do. With the Commodore uniform coat and silly hat hanging helplessly, one in each of Grace's hands, Jester marched by his lowly mate, casting the boat off himself.

As the Bullaks watched with amusement, the yacht pulled away from the pier, but Grace's humiliation had been made quite clear. As they sailed out of Brisbane Harbour and its flotilla of pleasure boats, bobbing peacefully in the bay, the yacht sailed spritely through calm waters. The winds billowed out the white sails like angel wings, and Grace's curling dark hair was stirred by the sunny, wind-blown air. She decided to forget the embarrassing incident, and as she watched her boyfriend Jester step into the cabin to take the wheel, she remembered how much she thought she loved him despite his past history of broken promises. She tried to forget her old love Sean Hope, who proposed to her on one knee when she was but a girl. She fought from crying at the brief thought of him, wearing a black and white missionary coat, as he tried to teach the children in her African Swahili village of Jua the *Lord's Prayer* and the *Hail Mary*, so many years ago.

Instead, Grace decided to get on with the voyage, and as she stepped toward the bow to trim the sail, she concentrated on her job as well as trying to forgive Jester. She remembered Afterall, he helped her with a visa to get into Australia, and gave her this job as trainee mate and waitress. It paid so little she could barely afford to pay the rent for her small flat in Brisbane. But she was eternally grateful to him despite her desire to start a new life without the miserable clown that led a life of sin.

Chapter Two

In the early afternoon, the calm waters turned choppy, and the strong winds coming from the south now uncertain. Storm clouds grew tall overhead and Grace looked up, her face growing worried. Still embarrassed due to her earlier argument with Jester, she watched as he marched onto the deck from the cabin. She was ordered to trim the sail again as the wind spun around to the north, and the tell-tale arrow on top of the main mast turned into the growing wind.

"Grace, GRAB THAT ROPE!" Jester barked.

She tried to comply, but a wave hit the yacht, and she slipped onto the deck floor. As the sailboat rocked, Grace heard Carliss squeal from the ornate table on the other side of the deck: the tourists' gooey lunchtime fare had covered their TV costumes in gobs of whipped cream and strawberries, stuck even into Carliss's stringy blonde hair. Then, the replacement Champaign flutes which Grace had reset, as well as the table, were blown over the side of the tossing yacht. Our heroine watched as Huxley the Naval Commodore staggered to the railing, vomiting his lunch into the wailing void, his green face stating that he didn't much like sailing.

Jester screamed at Grace as she got back to her feet, fumbling with the ropes: "You should know how to do this!" he yelped. "You've had enough lessons from me. You should know the Lost Lovers from stem to stern by now."

"You gave me only one lesson!" Grace retorted with a voice like thunder. "How dare you give out to me!" and she turned again to the wayward sail.

As the boat rocked again, Jester ran toward the cabin. But when a stronger wave hit, it knocked him right over, covering him in a blanket of thick snow-white sea foam. Grace stepped into the cabin. As she peered inside, she saw the wheel spin and realized the boat was out of control.

When she staggered back out onto the deck, the yacht yawed again, this time tipping toward the mad ocean. As the gunwale dipped into the storm-tossed seas, the ocean drove over the side, the deck now awash with white water. Jester struggled to get to his feet. But he was shocked as Grace raced by him, toward the wheelhouse cabin again, determined to gain control of the Lost Lovers and get her back on course.

"What are you doing?" Jester screamed, disgusted with his only crew member. "Leave that wheel to me, and don't you dare take control. That's the Captain's job! I'll turn her west and we'll be fine in just a moment or two."

"But that's madness!" Grace shouted despite her boss's stern look, and she pointed a steady finger into the storm. "Turn her west and we're dead! Look at those waves. They're as high as a house and will break us in two with such deadly force, we're all sure to drown! But look to the east. Why, the sun's about to come out. Turn her east and we're safe. It's our duty to save our guests, ourselves, and the Lost Lover, too."

"You're a BITCH, that's what you are," Jester wailed above the wind. "You leave her to me. Or you're fired! One, two, three!"

Then thunder crashed and lightning flashed. Grace ignored Jester as she sprang into action again. But the frightened Bullaks pushed past her first, racing into the wheelhouse and hiding under a bunk. There, they cowered in the shadows which were as black as a fallen, mythical dragon. Unperturbed, Grace raced in after them leaving her captain behind, more than a little perturbed that his only crew member didn't obey his order.

Chapter Three

Grace lunged into the cabin and grabbed the spinning wheel with both strong hands. It knocked her to the ground at first, but she got up and tried again, brave and calm even under extreme pressure and deadly weather.

Meanwhile, back on deck, Jester had managed to recover. He staggered into the wheelhouse, first seeing Grace at the wheel and then spying his guests crouching below in the deep shadows. But when he tried to move toward her to take command of his vessel, yet another wave knocked him over.

Still at the wheel, Grace tried yet again to hold the boat steady and finally gained control. Wresting it away from the forces of Nature, she fought the wind and strong seas and, as she did, looked through the salt-spattered front window. The frayed forward sail billowed full again, flapping and banging with the force of the storm. She knew the stress was too much, fearing the mast would let go. She pulled the yacht east, beginning to lose way, taking a compass heading opposite from the strong western storm and its hundred-knot winds. It was then that her face filled with pride because she sensed she had at last won and possibly saved everyone's lives.

Then, another roller hit, much taller than the rest. It again wrested the wheel from Grace's strong hands. The heavy wooden wheel spun out of control yet again.

And when she tried to grab it, why, a wooden spindle knocked her on the chin, throwing Grace against a far bulkhead steel bin.

That's when Jester saw his chance to recover from his humiliation. Stepping over Grace now sprawled, unconscious, on the deck, he ignored her completely as he smiled bravely at his tourist guests. Jester's face was still white with terror, unlike Grace who looked completely under control despite still being unconscious and dead to the world.

"I've got it!" he shouted to no one above the dying gale. And as the boat turned south toward Brisbane's fair harbour, the sun finally came out.

For you see, Grace was right all along. Had Jester turned toward the storm when the gale had prevailed and into the seas awash with white water, he would have sunk the Lost Lover for sure. Yet because of Grace's right thinking, the crew, guests and yacht sailed into the sun and fair weather, and back to the safe harbour of Brisbane, on Australia's northern border.

Chapter Four

After Grace had saved the lives onboard the Lost Lovers and sailed back to Brisbane with the yacht, she tied her to the pier and cleaned up the mess as Jester and the tourists sat with pasty faces, recovering in the sun. Later, my dark-skinned friend came over to my home and we sat on the patio. We looked out over Brisbane Bay, the evening sky now as dark and as silky as Grace's skin. The harbour glistened with the full moonlight on that balmy night as I studied her face which, though black, I thought of as my only real kin.

As we finished eating at an outdoor table, my husband Bill, seventy-one years old and a mere boy who was twelve years younger than me, cleaned up after dinner. As he carried the dinner plates and wine glasses into the house, he left us alone and I hoped Grace would confide in me about the upsetting voyage. I knew it had been difficult just by looking at her: Grace's eyes were all red which could only be from crying following the harrowing voyage and a fight with Jester, because the African couple who had hauled the tourist trunks had told me about it, and I'd seen it all before. Grace's face was still streaked with white trickles of salt which could not be from a storm but from tears coming from both anger and embarrassment. At her silence, I cleared my throat and moved my chair closer.

"I don't understand what's gotten into you," I observed, sitting back in my seat. "I've known you since you emigrated here from your small African village. You keep telling me you're Swahili – that's a confident tribe. I *know* you were imbued with the same courage your people and strong warriors have. After all," I sniffed, "they had revolted against the dreaded British to retake their land."

But my strong observation and outburst was met only with Grace's silence. I leaned forward in my chair, looking my friend dead in the eye. "Grace, what's bothering you? Isn't there anything I can do?" But Grace only shook her head.

Suddenly, the peaceful night was disturbed as I rapped loudly on the glass patio table.

"Enough of this nonsense. I'll tell you what. That man you work for, that Joking Jester. You tell me you're dating him but he's a CLOWN! He abuses you and embarrasses you and tells you what to wear and what music to listen to and how you should dance and he wants you to cut your beautifully black and silky long curling hair. Don't you see, he's destroying you? Can't you listen to me?"

But Grace only shook her head again. I pushed back in my chair. It grated on the flagstone patio as I stood up tall.

"Then I'll give you one last chance. You're my best friend, in spite of our age difference, backgrounds, and colour of our skins. You leave Jester before it's too late and I've lost the intelligent woman, my friend, whom I've come to love and respect. It's your choice, Grace. Leave him or I'm afraid I'll never talk to you again."

As Grace looked up in surprise at my uncharacteristic outburst, I turned my back and stormed into the glittering night.

Grace finally stood up, and the moonlight glistened on her bare arms as she hunched her shoulders in fear. Tears streamed down her face as she contemplated my strong intuition: an insight Grace remembered she had once possessed, too. She realized she had been wrong to trust Jester even when she had first met him. She should have learned something by now. The deadly voyage had only confirmed what she had known all along – that I was right and he was out to destroy her and she should leave him right now! Jester the fool was only a Clown and much too unworthy for Grace who was as good as a saint, and just as holy and sound.

Chapter Five

Later that night, Grace paced her one-bedroom flat that she couldn't really afford. A pile of envelopes rested unopened on an old wooden kitchen table. She already knew what was inside each one:

A final demand from her mobile phone and Internet provider, which gave her the means to keep in touch with her mother back home in Africa; a first demand for the University tuition she was paying to complete her final year toward two Master's degrees, one as a Psychiatric Doctor and the other as a Theology Teacher. And the most worrying one of all: in a brown paper envelope, a snotty letter from her landlord instructing her to get out of her flat even though she had nowhere left to go.

All remain unpaid due to the small salary Jester gave her. Walking to an open window, she stood silently, gazing out on the full moon that still glittered off of the Bay's still waters. She remembered how, just the other day, in the snug lower bunk of the Lost Lovers, and having been forced to have sex with the Clown, she had asked her so-called boyfriend for a raise. He had ignored her completely even though she had confidentially shared the financial embarrassment she now faced. Grace even told him about her abusive landlord and how he had shouted at her, threating her with eviction if she didn't pay up.

"Can I stay here, onboard our lovely yacht? Jester, I've nowhere left to go if the landlord throws me out, as is his right because I've not been able to pay him in months."

"What do you mean *your* yacht. It's mine!" Jester snarled as he got out of bed.

"But you said we'd soon get married," Grace cried, tears streaming down her face. "Which means that everything I have is yours and everything you have is mine, including our hearts and the sailboat. Isn't that what you promised?"

"I never promised any such thing," Jester snarled again as he used a hand to wipe his mouth, removing her lipstick, evidence that he did not want his English guests to see after forcing her to have sex. "We'll talk about any promises tomorrow."

But seeing the look of worry and disappointment on Grace's beautiful ebony face, he sat down again. When she saw the look he gave her in return, of sorrow and apology for what he had done, she knew that despite her dislike of him he truly loved her.

"That landlord sounds as raucous as an out-of-control dinosaur, and as loud as I am, which means he didn't really mean it," Jester quipped as he slipped on his swimming trunks, getting ready for a dip in the Brisbane Marina waters. "Tell you what, Grace. You see, I'm a little short of cash this month. Next month should be better because more wealthy tourists are due in on the chartered airplanes from

London and America. Stop worrying. I'll take care of you. Isn't that what I've always promised?"

But Grace knew he was lying. He had never, ever kept the promises he had made to her. Not even one.

With that, Jester marched up the steep steps to the yacht's deck and, leaving her alone, Grace finally cried about the terrible mistake that she had made when first emigrating to Australia. Jester was impossible but when she had first met this circus Clown, she had absolutely no choice but to accept his proposal of marriage or she would have never received her Australian visa and would have been deported. Yet she still hated herself for having sex with Jester. While she had made love to Sean when she was only sixteen, and though she liked having sex, she knew making love to Jester was a sin and against the morals her mother had taught her.

***

Still standing at her flat's open window, Grace woke from the waking nightmare, and recounted how she had unconsciously looked back on the way she was living. Her face covered in sweat and tears, she was now fully conscious. Outside, she saw through the window how Brisbane Bay now glimmered only with starlight. Hours had passed, the moon had finally set, a moon that had always reminded her of her mother, Luna, who lived far over the horizon. Now Grace was alone once again.

With tears in her eyes, she closed the window. Then she again remembered Sean, her lost lover, and how he had made love to her (it was the very first time) when she was only sixteen and he but a lad of eighteen. She had loved him so much she had chosen him to be the very first man to touch her full breasts.

Chapter Six

Sean Hope was only twelve when he began helping the poor in his native town of Advent, a rural town just outside of Detroit, Michigan. As he grew older, he spent his Thanksgivings, Christmases and Easters, too, down at a breadline right next door to Detroit's Metropolitan Zoo. On the cold winter nights, with stars sparkling bright, and as the animals roared, he'd distribute hot turkey dinners, soup and sandwiches to those who could not afford even a single slice of bread, much less two. Then Sean made sure each one had a warm, snug bed in the large Catholic Church sanctuary, heated to keep out the cold of the harsh winter night.

His Roman Catholic Parish, St Thomas of Assisi, was impressed by the young man's enthusiasm and caring ways because he spent all his time with the poor rather than play baseball, his friends' biggest interest. So impressed was the Archbishop that, when the time came, he agreed to pay full tuition together with room and board at Notre Dame in the state of Indiana, the nation's renowned Catholic University. The Archbishop had long thought the young man might be his successor, but when he told the young man of his decision, the older reverend saw that Sean was torn.

"Archbishop," Sean said shyly, "I always believed that when I grew up, I'd like to be a writer like Hemingway. I want to write like that great novelist wrote, about lions and marlins and all that adventurous stuff."

But when the Archbishop pointed out how Sean could help the poor as well as write, the young man agreed that the poor and homeless came first because it just felt right. It was a decision that plotted the course for the rest of young Sean's life.

Little did he know that his decision to feed and minister to the poor would lead him to a young woman he would fall in love with, a love so strong that he would buy a large diamond engagement ring and propose marriage to her after only a few days.

A few months before his first classes at Notre Dame, a priest – his sociology teacher – suggested he go to West Africa, there to understand at first-hand what world poverty looked like. So, Sean packed his bags and took a long flight, ending up in a foreign African east-coast city because the plane's engines had overheated and were as hot as burned toast.

While he waited in the terminal for a flight bound west to his final destination, he read a pamphlet about the Swahili people and their amazing location. He read how their nation sat along the Indian Ocean, and the word 'Swahili' meant 'The People of the Coast'. Fascinated, he changed flights and Sean Hope never looked back but instead his heart filled with hope. But then the unexpected happened for, only the next day, he would meet the young girl of his dreams who swept away his soft heart and little did he know as he boarded the plane that she would soon feel the same way.

***

Meanwhile, Grace – now only sixteen and about whom I, Kylie Whipple tell this story – was out on the savannah with her own animal zoo where nothing but tall grasses ever really grew. Giraffes and lions and monkeys and apes gathered 'round her each Sunday and, like Saint Francis of Assisi, whom Sean's parish was named after, Grace had a giving heart who's loving beat made the animal's hooves thump pitter-patter.

When she got home to her village Jua (which means 'Sun' in English), she was met by the children who acted just the same as her zoo of savannah animals. They'd gather 'round her in a vast circle of love, because they really loved Grace who was as kind and as soft as a turtle dove. And before they slept each night their own female 'Saint Francis of Assisi' would read them a story in the soft Swahili moonlight.

That Sunday, when Sean arrived at a regional airport not so far from her village, Grace had no idea that her young life was about to change. She was studying her Bible as was her wont for even though she was young she could quote scripture. Her favourite, of course, was St Francis's quote: "Lord, make me an instrument of your peace. For where there is hatred let me sow love, and where there is sadness, let me make joy."

Not bad for a Swahili kid just sixteen years of age.

As for Sean, having decided to fly to the airport nearest to the Swahili location, he found himself studying a map when he noted a village with the lovely name of Jua that struck his imagination. He thought how it would be nice to take a break in the sun, and though he did not know that Jua meant 'Sun' in English, he took a crowded bus filled with villagers and other tribal members whose homes were near the Indian Ocean, riding on top with many of them until their journey was done. And that's how he got to know them. Right there on the spot, covered in dust and soot and tears of laughter he had shared with his new friends, he decided that Jua would be his final destination.

It was a Sunday and sunny, still morning when Sean at last arrived and he walked through the neat village of Jua where he witnessed so much pride. Each home and building was as neat as a pin. Just like the families that lived there, the houses suffered not one little sin. At their front doors, some male and female villagers gathered together with their many children, and Sean saw how some of their arms, legs, faces and chests were tattoo'd with African symbols like bright badges of honour.

As Sean walked along the main, dusty thoroughfare, he saw other villagers enjoying themselves, talking and gossiping as the females of the tribe planned dinner. Then the Church bell was rung and the villagers, both male and female and their children and grandchildren, walked in a line toward the small village church. Sean followed them to Mass and when he got there, knelt in a pew and said his prayers with them. As they prayed together, he glanced sideways, this way and the other, and saw how their skins were as dark as chocolate and as rich as homemade peanut butter.

Then, as he saw the priest walk up to the altar, his eyes fell on a young woman whose glowing black eyes flitted toward his. And for a moment they locked as if in an eternal kiss.

***

After Mass, in a wooden building nearby, Grace gave Sunday School lessons to a classroom full of normal and mentally disabled kids. Sean asked her if he could listen to the children as they stumbled, trying to learn their prayers, like the *Act of Contrition*. Sean was impressed. The *Act of Contrition* is a long prayer. But all these kids were smart because they were almost there. But despite their verbal trouble Grace coached them on. She coached them by writing down each word on a blackboard behind her and Sean was even *more* impressed – not only with Grace's patience as they tried to get their tongues around the long words, but the simple fact that these children from such a remote village – kids that some might call 'stupid' – could read every long word.

When Grace was finished, Sean strode to the blackboard and, by her side, spelled out the words for the *Lord's Prayer* and the *Hail Mary*, simple prayers but important to their Catholic religion.

"These are the most important prayers to learn," Sean said to the kids as they looked at him with round eyes. "If you can learn the *Act of Contrition*, you can certainly learn these simple words because you're more than smart – you're all so intelligent it actually makes me smile with a leaping heart."

As they started, the children's tongues twisted and turned as they tried out the new words, but they didn't find the prayers at all hard or complicated.

"Our Father," one child said as she tried on the two words. "Who art in Heaven," she continued. Then the rest of the kids took up the prayer.

"Hallowed be thy name…"

When they had made it to the end of the prayer, Sean was surprised that they had already learned it by heart! "…but deliver us from evil, Amen."

"That's one Great Amen," Sean whispered to Grace. "Now why don't we try the *Hail Mary*?"

That prayer was even simpler to learn because it was approximately one quarter of the length of the *Lord's Prayer*.

When they were finished, and after the rest of Sunday School where Grace talked them through the Priest's Sunday sermon, and the children had all streamed home to their parents, Grace invited Sean to dinner at her simple home because there were no restaurants in such a remote village as Jua. So, they walked down the road to her house where Grace introduced Sean to her mother, Luna, in the afternoon sun.

When Sean asked a few questions, like: 'How can you possibly survive in such a place so distant from a town or city, without Internet or cell phones or even a broadcasted musical ditty?' Grace laughed as Luna explained.

"Why, we make our own music, Sean, is that so surprising? We're taught from our traditions – it's as much a part of us as the sun rising and our old superstitions."

Then she broke into song, Grace quickly picking up the close harmony, and soon men, women and children standing on their doorsteps joined in:

Wageni wako wapi, twataka kumuona? *

Visitors, where are you, we need to see you?

Kwanza tuwaone, pili tuwasikie, tatu ni vitendo, ya inne ni furaha.

First we see you, second we hear you, third comes action, fourth comes joy

Chorus - Iye ni wema iye - *Oh yea, it's good, oh yea.*

Shule ni wema – *school is good* / Mambo sawa – *things are good*

* Hear the closely-knit singing of the Swahili as they sing Wako Wapi?

When the people of the village were finished singing, after Luna had served a simple dinner of Piri chicken and a pot of Jollof Rice, Sean and Grace took a stroll to the savannah where Grace took delight in introducing him to her personal zoo, not only the ones we've previously met, but a giant elephant too! And Sean was scared to death!

Having gotten over his shock, they walked back to Grace's home in the setting African sun.

When it became obvious that Sean had nowhere else to go, Luna invited him to sleep in a hut not far from their home's porch. Following a simple snack of leftover rice and chicken, Sean said his good nights and tread to the hut oh so very, very slowly because he was dog-tired. As the moon rose on that magical village night, he found himself praying for Grace whom he had known for only hours. After that, he made up his bed with a blanket of hay because the hut also acted as Grace's animal shed and the sheep put him to sleep with their chorus of 'Ba-ha-ha-haaa's! which reminded Sean of the children singing. Later that night, with the moon shining bright, Sean woke to find that he'd been dreaming of his beautiful new Swahili friend. What he could never guess was that Grace had been dreaming of him, too, and how he would one day propose to her in marriage and not a moment too soon.

Only three days later, the pair (which Luna now considered a couple), strolled arm and arm through the savannah's long grass. On that hot afternoon, not even a lion stirred. It was then that Sean said what he had longed to say. He took Grace by the hand and looked deep into her eyes.

"Grace, you'll think me a fool. But I've fallen in love with you."

Her dark face was taken with a look of surprise. "But don't you see my dear Sean?" she said. "I love you, too."

The pair knelt and kissed and embraced. Then they made love because they'd found each other not a moment too soon. Each was ready, each knew what to expect. They were as certain of each other as a lioness is when she lovingly licks her new kitten until it's perfectly wet.

***

The next morning, still asleep in his bed, Sean received a telegram, hand-delivered by a young villager, from the Archbishop who had been trying to track him

down across West Africa, which was much more complex than learning calculus. Sean had been expected to meet a church delegation at Sir Seewoosagur Ramgoolam International Airport, his original destination. They were surprised because he had never shown up, and had called the police instead.

Furious with his young protégé, the Archbishop recalled Sean to Notre Dame, there to start his theology class. When he received his Prelate's telegram, and now in a rush, Sean ran to find Grace to share with her this troubling news that would prove to interrupt their young newly-found love before it had really started.

Seeing her outside the village church, he got down on both knees and said, "Oh my sweetheart, you are everything to me. I know that in time we'll have many children in our home's loving nest. Please, my beautiful one, will you marry me?"

Then he gave her a small box, begging her to open it. When she did, she found a glittering diamond ring that flashed in the sunlight, sparkling into her eyes, and Grace knew it must have cost her love a fortune, more than he made in three years of ministry devotion. She wondered how he had found the money and when Sean saw the question in her dark eyes, he told her he had taken a bus in the dead of night back to the city. There he had found a jeweler in the square, had woken him to make the purchase, and had phoned his bank to have the cash wired from his savings account back in America to a financial institution in the Swahili city. That's how he had paid for her engagement ring. When he said that, Grace knew he had tapped his entire fortune, the one he had saved for his future and to feed the poor, and to help heal the sick by paying their doctor bills.

"You're a fool, Sean, don't you know it, and I'm breaking up with you right now!" she threatened. "I'd never marry a fool or ever be with one. Don't you know that? Don't you know yet what kind of woman I am?"

Grace closed the box and slung it high into the air where it landed at Sean's feet, buried deep in the village sand.

"Please, Grace," Sean begged. "Come home with me to America. You can go to University to study theology and psychology if that's what you want to do but you'd be good at anything you turned your hand to, not like me. I'm only good at writing and helping those who can't help themselves."

But as he said it, Sean realized by her face that Grace would miss her African family and the friendly animals in her zoo, too.

"But Sean, that's impossible," Grace said, with fire in her eyes she was so upset. "I'm Swahili not American. What would I do? No one in my tribe has ever gone to college much less left home. So why would I ever go with you?"

But Sean was not only in love, he was also dead smart.

"Grace, you don't see it but your mother does and even I do. Not only are you super intelligent but you can connect with the mentally disabled much better than most doctors. Didn't I just see you teach a school filled with kids a complicated prayer like the *Act of Contrition?* You were so patient, writing on that blackboard, they sopped up your teaching like a sponge.

"Not only that but I'm convinced the Archbishop will pay for your room, board and tuition, too."

It was then that Sean saw Grace's black eyes fill with tears as deep as African night skies. He realized she could never leave her tribe. He watched as she withdrew her hand and turned from him, dashing back home, and he knew he'd lost his only love forever.

After Sean returned to Grace's home, and admitted to Luna that her daughter had broken up with him, he went back to his hut to pack. Then he wrote a small note to Grace and, placing it in the box with the glittering diamond, buried it deep in the sand outside her hut where he knew his lost love now slept. Then he went to sleep in his usual place, covering himself with cold hay. The next day, he took the bus back to the city, and there he climbed on the plane.

On the flight back to America and an uncertain future, he prayed to Our Lord that his love was not gone forever, but only misplaced like a forgotten love letter.

Meanwhile, in her hut and unable to sleep, and having paced the floor for hours as she regretted her anger and what she had said to Sean, Grace looked out her open window at a moon which had always reminded her of her mother. It was a full moon and as she watched storm clouds marched in, covering the moonlight completely, dousing it like a candle going out. Then the wind came up from the south, and the grasses outside her hut swayed, pointing directly north. The soughing voice of the grass seemed to Grace to be talking to her, telling her the time had come to be a grown-up woman, and it pointed directly north. The magical song reminded her of the Saint of India, Mother Teresa, and how she had taught and healed the poor. Grace made up her mind and packed a small bag filled with only enough to survive for five days, the time it would take to travel to India where she hoped to become a novitiate to the renowned Mother Teresa. She looked in her purse and found only enough money for her passage.

As she left the hut for what she thought might be the last time, because she had no idea when she would be back, she looked in on her mother asleep on her matt. Grace found a paper and pen and wrote a note telling Luna not to worry, and gave her the address of Mother Teresa's Missionaries of Charity in Calcutta. Then she crept from her home and past the barn where she knew her lost lover slept. Little did she know that Sean could not sleep either, so worried was he about the words he had spoken to her, and knew that Grace would be the only love he would ever have in his entire life.

Grace wanted to go in to wake him and apologise for the terrible argument and hold him and make love to him again, but instead she headed toward the village's only bus stop. There she waited as dawn broke over the savannah, and saw how the skies were again as clear as a vast blue ocean. She could hear the singing of the early birds as they greeted a new day, and for a moment she thought of not leaving. But when the bus came and she climbed aboard, she vowed to herself never to look back.

When she arrived in Haldia, a busy Indian Harbour, she made her way to

Calcutta by bus just like Sean did when he first came to her village, though she did not know that because they never had time to discuss it, they were so busy getting to know each other and finally making love. When she got off the bus, she asked directions to the Mission and, walking through the crowded streets, couldn't believe the number of people. She had never realized so many people could walk on one single street, and realized that millions walked on every street of God's Earth.

When she managed to find Mother Teresa's blessed house, the Mission, she entered it and found her new Mother surrounded by other young women who also sought a vocation as novitiate or apostolate. But the Reverend Mother, who looked like a Saint, explained that life as a Nun was not all wine and roses. She sat down amongst them, and taking out her glasses, lectured them on what it would be like to work with the poor of Calcutta.

"One evening a gentlemen came into our house and said, 'Mother, there is a Hindu family, a single mother who is our neighbour, and her children have not eaten for a long time. Please do something for them'," said Mother Teresa. "So with my fellow sisters, I took many bowls of rice and went immediately to that home and there was the single mother, and behind her stood a group of little ones and five little faces who were her children, and their eyes shone bright and their bellies stuck out due to sheer hunger. The young woman took the rice bowls from my hands; she divided them and went out with half the bowls stacked in her arms. When she came back without them, I asked her: 'Where did you go? What did you do?' But she refused to tell me. Much later, I learned that half the food had been given to the family next door, a family which had ten children. When the starving next door neighbour ran from the front door to accept the meagre rations from the single mother, the crowds walking down the street saw them They rushed the poor family because they were all starving, too. In the ensuing riot fifteen people, including four children, were killed in the stampede and ensuing unquiet"

When Sister Teresa looked up at her new young charges, there were tears in her eyes. "We've not enough to feed even the starving. What can we do? We must raise more money. We must beg in the streets. We must distribute medicines. Yet, we have few resources and even fewer friends."

At that moment, Grace was given by God her true vocation in life.

"Mother, if you will allow me," she said, falling to her knees and taking Mother Teresa's hand. "Allow me to become a novitiate here. Let me go into the streets. Let me raise money. Let me distribute food and medicines. I do not want a salary. I do not need money. All I want is to follow my Lord's example of feeding those in need. Please, dear Mother, will you allow me to join your Ministry?"

It was two years later when tragedy struck down the young novitiate and Grace was raped in the streets by a gang of so-called English lords who called themselves gentlemen.

Having fled to India, and finding her life's vocation of giving to and helping the poor as her lost-love Sean had done so many years before, Grace took to the streets and like Mary Magdalene, Christ's wife to some, tried to survive by sleeping with men but that soon grew too tiresome. With nothing in her purse to survive on or give to the indigent, tired, or homeless, Grace hired herself out as a Jam Boy which meant she had to keep the flies away as the rich played golf and ate. To do so, she had to smear Jam all over her naked body, and when they finished playing golf they raped her repeatedly, her screams ignored by the other white golfers and Indian golfers too because, being black, she was considered an untouchable animal, like a pig or a sloth in an unwanted zoo.

Following the rapes, Grace was thrown into a room and the door was locked. And there she awaited her very dark fate, raped repeatedly until Sean happened by looking for her.

For years, Sean had regretted his decision to leave West Africa and his only love. And without asking the Archbishop's permission had left his studies at Notre Dame and booked a flight, once again using all of his money. When he walked into the village of Jua, he found Luna looking feint. She had not heard from her daughter in months, and worried at her young daughter's fate. Sean was aghast at discovering Grace had travelled to India, but was proud of her too, when Luna told him that she had joined Mother Teresa's Mission. He immediately booked passage on a freight steamer, using the last of his funds, and found his way to Calcutta. There, he looked for his love in all the crowded streets. He asked for her in the Mission, but Mother Teresa feared the worst because she had not heard from her young novitiate in many, many months.

Now more determined to find Grace than ever before, Sean tramped the busy streets of Calcutta every day and every night. And when he was just about ready to give up, on a dark night when his watch read that it was just past midnight, he heard a familiar voice followed by a tragic scream.

Having just raped Grace, a White Lord had left the door to a squalid tenement wide open, unthinking as he marched into the dirty bathroom to wash her sex off him, then showered. Seeing escape, Grace ran out of the door and began shouting but being an untouchable, the crowd in the street ignored her even though it was so very late. Starving and bleeding, she collapsed to the ground, which is when Sean found her. He picked her up, taking her in his arms, and he saw how she bled from her nose, mouth and around her beautiful eyes, and how her short white robe was soaked with blood at the crotch due to the many beatings and repeated rapes she had received.

He carried her back to his cheap hotel and cleaned her up, and took her off the drugs they had given her. Grace had become addicted to cocaine, you see, and they forced it up her nostrils so she could thrust and gyrate, going crazy with her beautiful body, to give her White slave masters better sex. When Sean found her she was almost dead and he took her to hospital.

When at last she recovered much of her health and could walk again, she bought a gun on the black market. She wanted to find the English 'gentlemen' who had raped her a hundred times each: eight of them in total but only one for which she could remember by name: Lord Ha-Ha-Ahem. She wanted to kill all of them but especially him because he had forced her to dance naked in the Calcutta streets. Sean convinced her to give him the gun, saying killing people was against the Fifth Commandment: Thou Shalt Not Kill. Grace finally put down the gun, having wanted to commit suicide and pointing it at her own temple. It was then, as Sean held her, that Grace remembered the lessons she had taught the children in her home village of Jua and the biggest commandment of all, The Golden Rule.

But she still would not go back to America, though Sean begged her to.

"Please, Grace, come home with me. In the United States I promise to protect you." When she shook her beautiful head, he got down on one knee again. "Then I'll ask you yet again: Will you marry me, my Grace? My only love?

She blushed at the proposal, her black cheeks turning pink. Then she blushed again and dropped to both knees to try to look in his eyes, but unable to she took his hand instead.

"Oh Sean, I'm so unworthy and I have sinned countless times. I must say No, though I will love you for the rest of my life."

He reached out with a hand and stroked her graceful face. Then he took out their ring, the One True Diamond Ring which he had dug up from in front of the door of her home and brought to India when he hunted for her, and Grace blushed again as she remembered how he had offered it to her so many months before.

"When I found you in India, do you know what I was told?" Sean said. "You took care of so many, the sick and the old; the young and the poor, the indigent and lonely; the homeless and beaten; and those who'd lost heart and needed your charity. You worked so selflessly, do you know what they finally named you?"

"What?" Grace whispered, not sure where this was going and fearing the worst. "What name did they give me?"

"They call you Saint Brigid, named after the Patron Saint of Ireland, and that's who you are. Every Tuesday, many in India say a Novena to you. You are an angelic, eternal, beautiful saint. A saint that has stolen my heart forever."

***

When, after Sean had found her, and she had returned to the Mission of Saint Teresa, Grace found that her Holy Mother was dying in her sleep.

"No!" Grace prayed to the Holy Spirit about Mother Teresa. "Holy Spirit, the Lord the Giver of Life, you gave Jesus his loving power to raise the dead like Lazarus. You let him walk on water. You let Him defeat death when He hung on the Cross, with six nails driven into Him: two through his hands, two through his wrists and two through His feet. Not to mention the spear they thrust into His side, or the crown of thorns they forced Him to wear, to pour blood like water down on His Holy Feet and upon his mother Mary and His wife Mary Magdalene, Peter and the Roman soldiers, and the crowd of spectators.

"Holy Spirit, let there be life in my Patron Saint, blessed Mother Teresa. Let your Holy Fires cleans her sins though she is as pure as the driven snow and as glorious as earthly air. Let her rise from the dead, for she is dead to the doctors, because her heart no longer gives out signals. Please, Blessed Spirit, let no harm come to her," pleaded Grace, who was holier even than the holiest of Saints.

But this time her prayers went unanswered, for reasons she could not explain. Sister Teresa of Calcutta breathed her last gasp and quietly passed away. And so it was that Grace's work in Calcutta was done before it had really begun. Instead of feeding the poor like her lost lover Sean, she crept back to him through the streets of Calcutta in the dead of night.

Finding his lowly apartment, she again slept with Sean at her side. But this time she would not make love despite his desire to do so. Instead, they fell asleep. A few hours later, woken by the guilt of the many sins she had committed, and in the dead of night, she left in the darkness and found a freighter that would give her passage to Australia. That's how she came to be in Brisbane, and that's how Grace, just like Sean, became the one who had abandoned her only love because she thought she had no choice even though she was so much in love with her lost lover, and this time thought she had lost him forever.

Chapter Seven

Still standing at her Brisbane flat's open window, dawn now filled an eastern sky. Haunted by her recollection of Sean, and with nowhere left to go and not knowing what else to do, Grace turned and packed one bag because that's all she owned – one single bag of personal possessions – then ran from her small apartment. She bolted to the Brisbane Marina, the dock deserted because it was so early in the morning and no one else was there — not one single person. All she could hear in the dawn's early light was the slow slap of the rising tide against the pier and the squawks of a flock of seagulls as they hunted mackerel for an early breakfast.

Having made up her mind, Grace quickly made her way to her employer's big yacht and untied the Lost Lovers from the pier. Casting off, she raised the sails because, despite what Jester the Fool had told her, she had learned exactly what to do.

In a fair early morning breeze, with her young heart singing and the wind in her dark hair, she stole the long sailboat like an early-morning thief and sailed north, bound for new lands and a life full of zest. Little did she know that she sailed toward an uncharted island and a zoo unlike any she had ever seen before. Nor did she sense that soon she would attend a Fish School in the deep, bright shiny sea, or watch, in seat 36B, a brand-new Animal Theatrical stage play, a play based in part on

Shakespeare's *A Midsummer Night's Dream*. For that, you'll have to read the next

Part, which is decidedly Part Two and not Part Three which is later in this novella.

Chapter Eight

For the next three days, Grace battled storm-tossed seas as one gale broke out after another, battering the Lost Lover yet again with high seas and nasty weather. Here, in the Southern Hemisphere, summer was quickly turning to winter. Yet on The Uncharted Island not far to the west, summer never ended because, like the musical Camelot, the would-be King, King Rex the 21st (not his real name, by the way. Rex thinks he's a tyrannosaurus but is actually a fat Hippopotamus), with his stupid wife Queen Doddy the 22nd, who believes she's Queen of the island but is actually almost extinct because she's a Dodo bird and would, by royal decree, not permit summer to set. (And a note from Kylie Whipple, your humble narrator: the other animals living on this uncharted island let this crazy pair think they were rulers, just to keep the peace. But in reality, they all laughed up their animal sleeves at the farcical act which these two would-be tyrants did their best to live up to and protect).

But back to the yacht: Exhausted and her courage used up, Grace had been horrified as the mast broke in two and all the sails were torn to pieces, the Lost Lover again almost sunk. But when the storms and high seas had finally abated, Our Heroine drifted upon a soft wind and spent her time recovering, asleep on the deck in the mild sunshine God had created.

On the fourth golden morning, asleep at the wheel, she did not feel the keel as it got tangled first in kelp, then became stuck in a harbour with a bottom of soft sand that did not hurt the yacht or Grace but only helped. Above the Lost Lover, the sun had come out yet again. When Grace woke, she crawled out onto the deck and beheld a magical sight: a single mountaintop peeked through wisping clouds high above her. And peering from a dense, lush green forest a troop of animal eyes stared out, like elephants, giraffes, monkeys, orangutangs, koala bears, glowing bees, and the glittering eyes of Sue, a Two Headed Roo, the mysterious island's only Kangaroo!

Chapter Nine

When Grace had partly recovered from her exhausting ocean fight by falling asleep below decks in the bunk she used to share with Jester the Clown, she stumbled back out onto deck and into the fresh afternoon light. Having rested for a spell, but still exhausted and shaking, she was startled by The Squawk of Birds and The Roar of Ferocious Beasts, then from the dark forest once again saw eyes peering out at her — the eyes of The Island's Mysterious Beasts!

Frightened at first, then more puzzled than anything else because The Beasts did not come onto the beach to investigate the intruder (Grace had long learned that beasts of prey investigate any animal that intrudes onto their territory but, of course, these beasts had never before been visited by humans so were as afraid of her as she was of them) Grace dove into the sea and, held by the warmth of The Deep Quiet Harbour, swam for land.

When her gracious dark feet stood at last on the golden strand, the island grew quiet at the human intrusion. Grace could hear a pin drop, so quiet it was. The only sounds that surrounded her were the gentle surf and the seagulls swooping high above. Tired from her swim and ocean fight, she began to lie down onto the warm summer sand. But then she again heard A Male Lion roar and The Monkeys chatter.

She realized they were angry and, springing from the sand, she ran to see what was the matter.

Running toward the dark forest and finally pausing to catch her breath, Grace leaned against a palm tree, accidentally disturbing a hive of Honey Bees dangling high above in an ornately built golden bee's hive which was also a bird's nest. Awoken, they dove down on her, forcing her to flee. Having not meant to waken them, Grace had no choice but to dash on in front of the angry swarm.

Forced to plunge deep into The Mysterious Forest, she discovered it was as dark as midnight which she had last experienced at her Brisbane flat's open window but without the benefit of The Full Moon's distant glow. Collapsing and now sobbing with fear, a bright light caught her eye as the sun came out, blinding her, despite the fact that The Forest hid her quaking fear.

'What a curious development,' thought Grace, between gasping breaths. 'How could the sun be out when the forest is so deep, there's not a crack between any Closely-Grown Leaf?'

Then, a sticky line seized her wrists. She was pulled further into the forest, at last falling into a bright silver spider's web which she could not escape from despite striking it with both closed fists. She screamed again in fear, struggling and twisting, but the web held her fast.

Caught in the web, she swung around to catch the shadow of something so large and frightening she quaked in fear again as it slunk through the forest in front of her. Grace sunk back into the web of the spider's bed as something monstrous

advanced menacingly toward her. A quick shot of red ink covered her face. She sank

into a trance, as a spider crept toward her on its eight hideous legs.

Chapter Ten

Grace woke, confused, no longer in the web. At her feet was an enormous rock and beside it, the handle of a small golden shovel stuck out of the sand. When she picked up the shovel and moved the big rock, she saw a dent in the ground that could not have been caused by any mere stone and scooped out a big hole with the shovel and her hands. To her astonishment, she found the Swahili bag of her childhood, which she had forgotten about long ago, and its African symbols of strength, love and courage. At its sight, she thought again of Sean, her lost lover. Pulling a small box from the hole, she immediately recognized it and smiling, opened it, somehow expecting to find the lost diamond engagement ring which he had given to her so many years ago. But instead, she found that the box held only golden sand.

Peering into it, she saw the edge of some paper. Pulling it out she discovered a note from Sean, wet with time and now almost illegible, one she had not seen on that night so many years ago when she had broken up with him outside her Swahili home, and he had gone back to America, and she had fled to India to begin her long journey. Grace pulled out the paper and saw it filled with Sean's careful writing, a note she had not seen on that night when she had broken up with him.

Slowly, she read what he had written to her all those years ago.

"My dearest Grace. I'll love you forever, no matter where you may go or what you may do. Our love is eternal, forever and ever, and forevermore. And one day, I promise I'll find you because I'll always love you no matter what you do."

Using crayons, he had coloured three hearts: two red ones meant for the happy couple and a golden one meant for the child they someday hoped to have, and which they had discussed the night they had first made love.

Her joy at finding Sean's note was interrupted by the call of Three Sea Horses who whinnied gayly and pawed the forest ground with their strong fins as if they were hungry and wanted to eat golden hay. One approached her by galloping over the beach, and saw to its dismay Grace wipe tears from her dark cheeks. As Grace watched, she witnessed a flash of light as the Sea Horses were magically transformed into human beings. The tallest of the humans was a large egg-shaped man who introduced himself as Bottom – and then introduced the other two who later, in the play-within-a-play which is part of *A Midsummer Night's Dream* which you, dear Reader, will soon get to enjoy, are cast as the mechanicals.

He introduced her to Mo – the plumber whom you will soon understand is a bit stupid too. He's the Man in the Moon in the Shakespeare classic. And then Bottom pointed to Bethanie – the carpenter and electrician, and smartest of them all, who is cast as the Lion in the play-within-the-play. But when Bottom spoke Grace did not answer and the lead mechanical and play's Director realised she did not understand him at all. He also realised she must learn to talk to the Animals and Fish if she was to find her misplaced lover Sean, whom you will soon learn was the giant monstrous spider as well as the Island's only Two-Headed Kangaroo.

Looking around the world for Grace, Sean had washed up on this mysterious island, just like Tom Hanks did in the film *Castaway,* when Sean's plane had crashed and he had not been able to sail on his life raft to any main land. Once on the island, he had been magically transformed not only into the spider but also into Sue the Two-Headed Roo, too! When he had arrived at his new home, Sean was relieved to discover that the island was not deserted but had any number of built-in friends. He had confided to all of the animals and these three magical humans too of how he had lost Grace, and still hoped to find her.

Ignoring Grace, who was clearly troubled by their mysterious appearance, the three human mechanicals huddled in a circle, and in another flash of light transformed back into the Three Sea Horses as, nearby, a group of fish swam toward the beach led by a White-faced Spotted Dolphin. Seeing the Dolphin, Bethanie encouraged Grace to get astride its back for an island tour, and the Dolphin took Grace around the glorious sparkling bay as the mechanicals and all of the other fish watched. As Grace dove and ducked beneath the Dolphin spray as it plunged through the waves, the mechanicals had a word with each other about how they should behave and what they might do.

"This lovely dark woman from the human world is the first to visit us ever," said Bottom to the others. "Did you see how she failed to understand us when we were talking to each other?"

"We'll have to do something about that," said Beth to Bottom so sweetly. "She seems a wonderful girl, if a little stupid, so let's send her to the deep."

"You mean to FISH SCHOOL!" shouted Mo to the others, brightly, not stupidly for a change. "There she'll learn to talk to us and to the other fishes and animals, too."

"And especially to Sean the Spider who is also our Two-Headed Kangaroo," said Beth to Bottom, so very earnestly. "Sean told me when he arrived here to this Castaway Island how, years ago, he had left her following her rejection of his marriage proposal. He found her in India, following the pillaging by the white and brown local men, who raped her repeatedly, and isn't that such a sin? To turn this wonderful woman into a jam boy, it really is horrible. But now, there's hope again! Sean told me how he still loves her, this saintly vision from Swahili-land. He wants to propose again but he's too shy to do so. But Grace has already found the note he wrote to her so long ago but not the diamond engagement ring. Sean hid that somewhere on our lovely island, but he's forgotten that because his memory is lost in the sands of time, too foggy to remember where he buried it. Maybe we could help him find it?"

"Not now," rumbled Bottom from his fat lips, wanting to move back to the previous subject. "First, it's Fish School for Grace, then we'll see about the engagement ring."

And as they watched, the White-faced Dolphin dived again, taking Grace to her first day of Fish School under the sea. As they watched, the mechanicals decided to plan the rest of that day's events. Now, dear reader, let's move on to what they planned together. A Celebration for Grace when she returns from Fish School! Now it's on to the next chapter.

Chapter Eleven

As Grace disappeared beneath the sea, firmly attached to the White-Faced Dolphin's back, the mechanicals, once again human, planned for a big celebration to mark Grace's return.

"Let's hold a parade and a fireworks display," offered Beth the electrician. "I've enough gunpowder to spark a huge rocket explosion."

"Nonsense!" cried Mo, the plumber. "I'll get a refrigeration unit shipped in from China. Those Honda units can make it cold enough to cover the entire island in twelve feet of snow. Our animal children can go sledding while the adults can practice slalom skiing taught by me, of course, so it's on with Grace's show!"

Bottom only grunted, the sound rattling his harry teeth.

"What do you know about skiing or sledding for that matter, Mo? And as for you, Bethanie," he cried, turning to his stage hand, "don't you think that fireworks would set the island's palm trees on fire? After all, I own a tonne of Palm Oil stock and earn interest and dividends every time that stock moves up due to floods or famines or even the outrages of war. Even I am allowed to make a living, simple mechanical that I am. And if I lose ALL MY STOCK due to a fire started by YOU, Bethanie, a mere speck on the nose of the mechanical race, how can I afford ANYTHING AT ALL? To eat, pay bills, pay my staff, feed the giraffe. It all takes money, don't you see that?!? In short: we've no fire equipment to put out such a huge blaze!" Bottom scratched his shiny bald egg head as he thought again about the predicament. "Mo, you mentioned a show, so… How about a play? What would you say to that?"

"What kind of play?" asked Beth. "I love Hemingway."

"Hemingway is a novelist," Bottom retorted. "While they've made many films such as *For Whom the Bell Tolls* and *The Old Man and the Sea*, novels usually make poor scripts for stage plays because most of them are too long, too detailed and can be somewhat laborious."

The mechanicals marched across the Golden Beach as they sought to think of what might work best to help them make ends meet and celebrate Grace's return. "I've got it!" shouted Beth. "But let me ask you a question first, and don't you dare break into a rage! Who is the Master of English writing for the Stage?"

"Christopher Marlowe, is that who you mean?" asked Bottom.

"No!" screamed Beth, triumphantly. "The Bard of stage-play writing himself and a Sixteenth Century icon and star. Why not something by William Tell, the bearded wonder who shows through actions while he tells through great dialogue as well!"

"Don't you mean William Shakespeare?" Mo observed smartly. "William Tell was the guy who shot apples off Bottom's banker's arse."

"I didn't know you were so smart, Mo, which makes quite a change," Bottom chuckled, then turned to Beth. "That's a great idea, Beth. Back when I attended university in the Great U.S. State of Illinois, I had a professor by the name of Mr Burda. He didn't call himself Doctor or any of that pretentious stuff. I well remember how, on our first day of class, he marched out onto the stage dressed all in black as if he was Hamlet himself. This well-educated man lectured to us: 'I'm going to make our Dead Bard Live!' And do you know what? That's exactly what Mr Burda did! Do you know we had to read the whole of Will's portfolio? Thirty-something plays in all. I had trouble with some of the playwright's works, especially *Pericles*, and came close to failing the exam. But Mr Burda told me that persistence pays off. So, I studied hard and got a B plus, one of the best in the class."

"Then that's perfect!" announced Beth. "But what play do you have in mind? Grace would LOVE *Romeo and Juliet*. I heard her talking to herself when she slept in the spider's web, under a trance created by Sean. It seems that play holds a special place in her heart because the theme of the play is about love lost then found again and then lost, but ultimately found when the two lovers — Romeo and Juliet — die in each other's arms. They're in Heaven together for sure! But my, it is a sorrowful Tragedy!"

"It's not a Tragedy," Bottom counselled. "It's a Romance disguised as Tragedy. In that way, Will got two plays in one! So why don't we make up a play we'll call *Lost Lovers*? And at its center one of the Bard's most famous magical comedies: *A Midsummer Night's Dream*?"

"That really is perfect!" Mo and Beth shouted together. "That way, we can again play the mechanicals on our wonderful stage that we can build if we work hard by night and by day. We don't even need light because the Moon is still full. Our island fireflies can supply glowing light, too, to act as theatre house and stage lights!"

"Then let us begin rehearsals immediately!" Bottom cried. "We'll gather our animals together while Grace attends Fish School. So, Hurry! Hurry! Before it's too late! Let's get going," Bottoms shouted, "and if anyone makes a mistake with the great playwright's dialogue, I'll borrow one of Beth's spiked high-heals and throw it at everyone's silly heads. Every member of the cast had better come to rehearsals prepared with their lines already memorized. Which means I'll have to write the play right now and cast it as we go along."

And that's how a play called *Lost Lovers* came into being, with a bit of Shakespeare's *A Midsummer Night's Dream* the central focus as a play-within-a-play, with a wonderful double meaning. It would be something unique and quite entertaining, and one of the two primary lessons of this part of our story. Once again, the writer of this spectacularly well-crafted book gets not one theme out of a novel, but two. Do you know what I meanan-ing?

("Okay, so the word 'meanan-ing'doesn't exist. But it does now!" grouses the writer of this novel *Lost Lovers*. "So, what if I can't spell? That's what Spell Check is for.")

Meanwhile in Fish School:

Grace again woke from a trance the fish had conjured to suddenly find herself underwater, clasping fast to the dorsal fin of the White-Faced Dolphin. She discovered that she didn't need air, instead she was in a bubble of oxygen that had been first released as a ring of silver by the Dolphin but which he broke with his beak. A zillion silver bubbles tickled her fancy so much so that she laughed. Then, coalescing like a galaxy of stars around Grace's sweet head, the tiny bubbles made one HUGE Bubble of O2 so big Grace could breathe without effort and started feeling excited, instead.

Away they all went, Grace and the Dolphin followed by octopi and Sea Horses and a legion of star fish crawling on their spindly bellies. Last of all was the Lobster, its claws opened wide, attached to the dolphin's strong flukes and its black and white hide.

"Ouch!" the White-faced Dolphin shouted. "Let go, Lobster. You're giving me a pain in my top-most fluke, all the way up to my vent!"

Grace's royal convoy tore through the sea, like something out of young Queen Elizabeth's original coronation but all in a frenzy. As they skated strong above the golden sands of a sea bed, a pirate named Hostin Duffman, who thought he looked like the famous actor Dustin Hoffman from the theatrical film *The Graduate* but not quite, appeared from behind a glittering curtain of sealight and tried to lop off a Sea Horse's head with his long Sword with all his might!

"Halt, Sea Horses," cried Hostin, a Swordfish with a VERY long sword. "Stop at once and surrender your gold or I'll chop ye into a million pieces!"

"But we're poor!" cried the Dolphin. "We're only escorting this human named Grace to our underwater Fish School. So why don't you join us if you've nothing to do?"

"But I've everything to do," groused the swordfish with a look of disgust on his long blue and white face. "I'm a pirate, you see. Can't you detect the Jolly Roger flag tattoo'd onto my tall Sail, you fool?"

Grace, who had not understood a word but interpreted the glaring look on the swordfish's face, took a careful look. She saw a black and white Jolly Roger tattoo grinning back from its sail, then studied Hostin Duffman with a difficult look.

"Is that what I think it is?" asked Grace. "A pirate dressed as a monstrous swordfish?"

"Pay it no attention," shouted the various fish that had come along to look at the ruckus and ignored the Swordfish confrontation. "It's not a he it's a her and she's harmless. Her name is EZMERELDA not Hoffman and she doesn't know if he's a him or a her or an it or a what. Her giant sword is only a banana if you really examine it."

Grace understood what the fish all shouted because the White-faced Dolphin, the only undersea creature who talked real English, interpreted the words for her.

When Grace looked, she saw that the fish and Dolphin were right. Rather than a body of silver and blue, Ezmerelda's makeup had melted off and all that was left of the sword was a drooping yellow toothless banana that grinned back.

"Why she's toothless too!" shouted Grace. "I'm tired of this. Please. Let's get to Fish School so I can really understand ALL of you!"

So away they all went like a sleigh-bed under tow. They dove lower and lower into the glimmering depths until finally they saw a dormant volcano that looked rather like a house from *The Hobbit* – who could have guessed? As they approached it, they could hear a bell ringing.

"Ding Dong!" the bell sang in its circular steeple. "Time to go to School for all the Fish who need learning. We're certain you're bored with the long summer recess and it's time to get back to studying!"

"Why, the School Bell even talks here!" Grace said with wonder in her eyes. "No, I can't understand it but I think I know what it's tolling. It's calling all the fish to Fish School. So, it's the first day of class?"

"That's right," said the Dolphin as he helped Grace to dismount and handed her two parcels with his fins. "Now here are your books and a packed lunch. Don't cry. It's all right. You'll be taken care of by a school mistress who's really a school man named Robin. I'll be back after school has ended to pick you up and take you back to our Magical Island and – so I've heard from the other fishes – for a celebration they're all having for you in honour of Grace's FIRST DAY OF FISH SCHOOL!"

And with that, Grace and the younger fish swam through the circular door of the Fishy School House. Though she was older than any of the other students, and while she had many degrees and much learning, she realised that these fish-kids could teach her a whole lot about language that she had forgotten. For such it is that when you lose a Lost Lover, your one true love, you forget almost EVERYTHING, even the love that he has in his heart for her, and she for him.

Or was the He a She, or maybe even a KANGAROO or a SPIDER? That's what we'll find out in our next glorious chapter.

Chapter Twelve

In the huge single school room of the underwater Fish School, Grace took a seat at the only human desk as many species floated and swam above her head. Then entered the School Mistress (or was it a School Man?), PETER PAN, who looked exactly like Robin Williams from the film *Hook*, an Academy Award-winning actor no one can ever resist and perfect to teach the animals and Grace new languages.

"Come to order, come to order!" the flying rascal, Peter, shouted. "Or I'll expel all of you right now before we even get started. Now, ELEPHANT RON, can you please take the rollcall to make sure every fish and every creature has shown up on this first day of Fish School?"

Grace looked closely at Elephant Ron, a huge floating pachyderm with great big flapping ears, and realized that he looked exactly like her old Jungle Teacher in Swahili-land who taught her to trumpet like the elephants and teach her students the English alphabet.

"Now don't you move while I take the names of all of you who've come to school," Elephant Ron said.

The pachyderm pointed at the underwater students with his pen, his narrow tongue sticking out and clucking as he called them by name. "Now Dasher, you

Prancing Seahorse, and Dancer, you wonderful Shrimp; then there's Comet, Hook's nephew, and Blitzen, the Star Fish's spiny cousin…."

As he continued his rollcall, other animals trooped through the door, each wearing HUGE BUBBLES OF AIR because they were kids from the Magical Island who'd been told to come to Fish School to learn how to talk to the Fish just like Grace.

"Oh, Morris!" called Ron to a baby Orangutang and his twin. "And Minnie, too! Why it's wonderful to have you twins at school. Oh my!" shouted Ron as Morris began to puke.

"Don't tell me your Mama already fed you? I told her not to because at noon today, we all get cookies and milk!"

As Ron and Peter cleaned up the mess with a water-vacuum, other Islanders began to crowd into the room. There was a tribe of Alpacas who helped to clean up by absorbing the droplets into their long woolen coats. And baby honey bees and a two-year-old monkey and even a spider who Grace thought looked exactly like the Monstrous Spider, who somehow reminded her of her Lost Lover (maybe it was the way his eight eyes shone at her, all of them filled with loving wonder)! But of course, Ron's rollcall was a very long list, so we'll skip to the start of this first day of class and leave out the rest.

Elephant Ron handed each student a pencil and a waterproof pad of paper and Peter told them they must write a journal each day to remember what they've learned and observed about each other.

"That goes for you, too," Peter called to Grace. "Of all of the students, you've the most to learn. You can't understand the animals at all, can you, except for the white-faced Dolphin?" he said, pointing to the rest of the class. Grace could only shake her graceful head and shrug 'Yes'.

They broke into groups, four at every watery table. Grace tried a few words of Fish-Australian, the local language. When the students started to laugh, Grace burst into tears and Ron the Elephant shook his long flapping ears.

"This will never do, will it? It's a sin to laugh at someone who tries!"

Then Peter chimed in.

"I'll laugh at each of you if you make a mistake, so no more laughing at Grace or each other. Getting things wrong the first time is a common problem. You have to learn *tolerance* to each other, which shouldn't be uncommon!"

As the day went along, Peter and Ron as well as the rest of the children did their best to teach Grace a thing or two about understanding *all* the fishy languages, from New Zealand to the far-off Atlantic, and as far away as the distant Aleutian Islands, and even the languages and cadences of the Magical Sea Island. For Grace quickly learned that, like the rest of the world and all of its Cultures, every Tribe has a language, dialect and accent all their own, just like the many regions and countries in Africa, her distant home continent.

Meanwhile, Back on the Magical Island:

The stage had been built and set for rehearsal. Bottom, taking command and marching out on the stage, then shouted, "Enter you animals and insects and anyone else who wants to be in our wonderful play!" and the extras all entered onto the stage, the honey bees, fireflies, monkeys, koala bears, giraffes, orangutangs and lions.

"I know why you've written *Lost Lovers*, and have a bit of *A Midsummer Night's Dream* as your central focus!" a tiny honey bee buzzed. "Sean, our Two-Headed Roo who is also the Monstrous Spider already told us! His love for Grace was all he had, and when he left the Swahili Village, he realized his departure was good and bad for both of them but especially for her, his long-lost lover. But even now he remembers the blessing Grace's mother gave to him as he walked out the door."

"What Blessing is that?" Beth wanted to know. "Do you mean Luna said the rosary with Sean? Because Grace says those prayers at every mid-day meal."

"Not on your life," a lion roared. "It's a hymn of redemption and we sing it like this:

'On the day of Grace's remembering, when she remembers to forgive herself for becoming a jam-boy to survive in India, not that there's anything wrong with

eating," the lion added. "She will come home to our island better than ever before and at last fully healed and forgiven. And then, on 4 October 2022, or is it 2023?, the day of Sean's birthday, Grace will notice her lover's dual duality, which are his two heads on the talking two-headed kangaroo. And on that day, she'll see not only his heads but his tall handsome tail that stretches to Heaven and all the way back to the island and her village Jua in Swahili-land, and all around the world and back to the beginning again! It is then that Grace will fully understand that Sean is not only a Roo and a Spider but her long-lost lover, too.

"And Sean will also change," the Lion continued, "because he will remember the words he wrote in his letter to her which he brought back from Swahili-land and buried somewhere on the island. But at the end of the mechanical's play-within-a-play, he will find the old letter and he'll re-read the words, and on bended knee he'll find the diamond ring he again wants to give her as he proposes to Grace his lover, and once again he'll seal his love with a kiss on her sweet cheek and a big hug that will make both of their hearts swell with forever happiness as well."

"And so it will all come full circle," hooted a monkey. "The lost lovers will have become found again to each other, just like our play, *Lost Lovers*."

"Which is why we'll make this stage play something awesome to behold while Grace is in Fish School learning to talk and understand the ocean's many fishes and animals on our island," said Beth, and held up her massive carpentry hammer.

"We'll build them a house made of lumber and a web of a bed made by spiders. It will hold their love together, like Super glue or duct tape, with a front door that will never be built wider."

"Nonsense," said Mo. "Let's build them a Wall, one so strong and true, to keep all those out that would sunder their glue."

As they argued Sue the Two-Headed Roo, who had found out only that morning that he must play both King Oberon and Queen Titania in our play-within-a-play and was dressed all in royal attire that looked like a Navy Commodore's uniform, hopped in on four feet, two of which were fake. (Writer's Note: Sean can be transformed from Sue the Two-Headed Roo to the Monstrous Spider and back to the Roo at the drop of a hat. But never will he again be a human until Grace, his one true love, recognises him.)

"What's this I hear?" said Sean aka the Roo and Spider, aka King and Queen Oberon and Titania. "You're planning a play? What's it about, we want to know, because we rule this magical island together with tyrannical King Rex and loopy Queen Doddy, who can't be here today, because they're sick of each other and have gone to sleep in separate beds." He glanced down at his royal attire that also looked like something from Gilligan's Island, the TV show, and thought a bit more about what he wanted to ask. "This morning when I woke, all I could find were these cast-away clothes from a yacht I've heard was sunk by the hurricane storm we had a few days ago, which brough my lost love to our magical island and back home. And I couldn't find Grace at all, don't you know!"

"My dear ruler!" Bottom said as he bowed, "let me explain it all to you before you die of stress and heart failure. First, let me say that Grace has gone to Fish School, and will be back by sundown. To celebrate her first day of class, we've concocted a play based on a writer and story you know all too well: *A Midsummer Night's Dream*, by William Shakespeare, not William Tell. We want you to play King Oberon and Queen Titania, and if that's not a hint, because I know you've read all of the great playwright and poet's works, *Lost Lovers* is written not just for Grace but for you, as well! And when we're done with our play, you'll both remember a secret within a secret, and by Thunder, all will be well. Therefore, sire, without trying to sound too bold, please just GET OUT OF THE WAY and OFF THE STAGE FOR NOW so I can get on with rehearsals!"

And with that, Bottom began rehearsing the play-within-a-play.

PART Three: Grace's Fish School Celebration and a Play-Within-A-Play

Chapter Thirteen

When darkness started to fall over the magical beach, crowds of elephants, tigers, koala bears, honey bees, fireflies, lions, giraffes, orangutangs, monkeys, and masses of fish swam in from the sea. They all converged on the stage that had been built without any delay and took their seats in the large circular theatre that had been built just for them. As the sun set over a cloudless horizon, and following a quick rehearsal during which all of the actors got their lines memorized and said them just right, Bottom placed the conch shell that he used as a megaphone against his fat lips.

"Oyez, Oyez, let all of you who are invited know that we now announce the start of the fabulous new show *Lost Lovers,* and it's opening night! Tamales, popcorn and drinks will be served at intermission, but for now QUIET ALL OF YOU so we can put on our extravaganza!"

With that, the house lights glinting from the backsides of fireflies doused while the curtain came up and the stage lights shouted!

"Quiet, you rabble in the audience," cried the fireflies brightly. "Listen to the bats that open our play with some fantastical memorable lines."

With that a bevy of bats flew out onto the stage.

"We begin our tale of love lost and found with a poem by Roo, the King and Queen of our Zoo!" squealed the bats who now hid in a tall belfry that acted as the fly space which glowed with the lights from a thousand fireflies. Sean hopped out costumed as the Queen and King and the Two-Headed Roo, too. He cleared his throat and, as he started his poem, his eyes darted around to look for Grace. She had been given a ticket for seat 36B but all Sean could see was an empty seat and his heart beat faster because she was not there.

"Heartbreak be to the lovers who voyage far from one another though they both believed at the time it was the right thing to do.

"Happiness be to those who find each other again, but have to circle the globe at least twice to do so.

"Happiness and heartbreak are our lot as humans of all races, and insects and animals and even the fishes that swim deep below the waves know that, too. For God wants us to find our own way, and many a mistake we must make before our ship docks at port, and home at last our hearts want to break no matter if we find happiness or heartbreak."

A trumpet sounded, and out marched a great BEAST, who glowered like Lucifer intent on a great feast. Then followed an ANGEL who looked like the Sun; from her brow sprang a rainbow like a multi-coloured holy halo.

"I'll not have ye happy," cried the Satanic beast as he shook a tall staff that looked like a prop used by Poseidon, the King of the Ocean, which was as tall as a skinny Giraffe. "I'll skewer you, Angel, with my pitchfork to make life miserable no matter what you might do."

"I fear nothing," said the Angel played by a female named Puffing McGee, the wife of singer Bobby McGee. "My halo stretches to Heaven that God may know my needs and wants and what it takes for me to be happy."

"And what is it you want?" asked Satan temptingly. "Long ago, near Jerusalem, when He trod the desert for forty days, I tempted Christ by offering Him up my darkly magical kingdom. Yet He only scoffed at me, the crazy chump. He wanted nothing of me, though I offered Him my soul in exchange for His own." He leaned toward the cherubic Angelic vision, his smile twisting in thistly Satanic derision. "How about a fair and Holy land where honey flows allllll the time. I'll make your insipid life last forever by penning a favourite nursery rhyme just for you, baby!"

"That doesn't rhyme," the Angel smirked. "To rhyme you must design the words in a pattern. It's a simple thing, Satan, but you've not the smarts to really matter. Your brain is as thick as Jiffy Peanut Butter!"

It glared at her, this Beast with No Name, and coughed like a fire-breathing dragon.

"Perhaps you would like fashion galore to replace your white dress with something much more appealing and fitting to this occasion?" the Beast continued.

The Angel tossed her head, the fake blonde curls shaking. "No Satan, that doesn't tempt me. I've dresses a-plenty, now can't you just see that you'll never sway me?"

"Well, what about a boyfriend, maybe it's just me? See sweetheart, my name isn't Satan, it's Goldie.ie, aka Goldilocks the three-headed one-thousand and ninety-seven-year-old dragon from Brooklyn, bound to snatch away all of Israel and that's not all! When I'm done, Oprah Winfrey and Ron Howard will want to make the film of *Lost Lovers*, staring – Guess Who? – Rabbi Goldie and that's me! Oh, and by the way, I'm the great-great-great-great-great grandfather of writer Tom Richards, the author of this novel of lost love, *Lost Lovers*."

With that, his Satanic countenance disappeared in a puff of smoke. When the

smoke cleared, the audience could see the three-headed comic, the infamous Goldie.ie made famous by Johnny Carson and his side-kick Ed McMahon. Each head held long whiskers, and side-curls that bounced up and down beneath a ragged Yarmulka he wore not only on the Sabbath but all the year round.

"You, my boyfriend?" the Angel cried as she stamped her golden feet. "Goldie.ie is a FAKE and so doesn't deserve to be with me. Be gone, you Satan, before you turn three zillion and thirty-three.

"I've Googled Goldie.ie," the Angel continued, "and while Goldie.ie might be real he's not related to Tom Richards, nor is he as talented nor as rich as that no-so-famous novelist."

(Note from this writer to the Reader: see for yourself by going to this author's Facebook page, www.tomrichards.ie that Goldie.ie really is real though he rarely shows up anymore! And though Goldie.ie doesn't look like this author at all, he's stolen my pictures and videos, and uses Adobe production skills to make it look so very, very real! But beware of Goldie, because surely, he is a fake. And though the Angel states that this writer is rich, I'm anything but, yet I agree with her: I'm not so famous.)

"On Facebook, Goldie.ie keeps saying that Tom Richards plagiarizes Hemingway, but that's only a lie!" the Angel continued. "Richards is talented, and don't I know why? My real name isn't Angel, it's Carmel Murray don't you know. I'm the inspiration behind the creation of everything Tom writes. From *Dolphin Song* to *Always Come Home*, and to Tom's forthcoming novel *Joe and Jane Me*. And even to this novel – this *Lost Lovers* – about happiness and heartbreak which is this loving couple's lot, too, because Tom and I planned to be married last Easter but then I got sick and we've not seen each other in months, which is why we are also Lost Lovers, just like Sean and Grace, a misfortune which many couples face across this good Earth before they at last find each other before it's too late! And I'll tell you what, before you get taken offstage by Captain Hook acting on behalf of Bottom," Carmel said sweetly to Goldie.ie, "I'll kiss each of your three noses just so you can say you knew me before we all became famous!"

With that, Carmel aka the Angel aka Mrs McGee, kissed Goldie.ie's three noses, then turned to the audience and delivered an aside: "Golde.ie copyrighted and trademarked by Tom Richards but NOT Storylines Entertainment Limited because it's ALL A FAKE! The management, including Frank McQuaid, the transport and promotions VP, think they thought of Goldie aka Golde Meir, the prime minister of Israel, even though Golde.ie thinks that Israeli Prime Minister is still alive! But Goldie was Tom's idea all along and I provided the inspiration!"

With that, the curtain came down right on Goldie aka Satan's three heads!

"It's intermission time, it's intermission time!" the bees buzzed in unison. "Get your hot tamales and popcorn at a special offer price of three when you buy two, an offer created just for you! And if you buy five you get one free plus an entire Free Zoo!"

And with that, the stage lights went out and the houselights went up, and the audience stretched preparing for Act II.

And so it is time, dear Reader, to begin Act II which is a play-within-a-play featuring *A Midsummer Night's Dream* by the greatest Bard of all time, William Shakespeare! And it stars *not all* of the animals on the Magical Island but only a few of the less famous ones. It certainly does NOT star Goldie.ie nor Satan nor any other animals in those infamous dark islands located far below the horizon and in the hottest spot in the centre of the Earth. So, sit back and finish your drinks (why not a Mojito with crushed lime for something very, very special?), then put up your feet and let the show go on!

"Billow, billow!" sang Bottom's sweet horn. "It's on with the play so don't go away! And now for our main act we feature the Night of Midsummer when all was not well, for romance was beset by a tragic tale. Shakespeare wrote it that way so he could get not one, but two, plays-within-a-play. We'll start here with two of the most famous lines from *A Midsummer Night's Dream,* and what are those lines, I ask? Why they're 'The course of true love never did run smooth', and 'And yet to say that truth, reason and love keep little company together now-a-days'."

"Isn't that what Will wrote?' croaked a frog sitting at the front of the house with his little tadpole child who had long ago stopped wailing. "Now on with the show before we start throwing our left-over tamales at you!"

With that, an Ape that had PROLOGUE spelled out on a HUGE CARDBOARD SIGN which he held staggered out from behind a fine flat to deliver in English as best as he could, the PROLOGUE from the play-within-the-play from *A Midsummer Night's Dream.*

"Frear not, or fi we offend, it is withourrrrr goodwill, That you should think we come nto to offfend, But with Goodwill. To show our simple skill…"

('And Man, is it Simple!' the Ape groused. 'We Apes chatter simply. But these men, then talk all ridiculously!')

But then he went on, having cleared his great throat and remembered to think before he pronounced the English lines and what the Bard wrote.

"…That is the true beginning of our end! The actors are at hand, and, by their show, You shall know all that you are like to know!"

As the Ape left, he handed the PROLOGUE SIGN to a character named QUINCE who is played by writer Tom Richards in disguise because he also acted as Quince at Illinois Wesleyan University back in nineteen-seventy-seven when we were all that much younger.

"Gentles, perchance you wonder at this show. But wonder on, till truth make all things plain. This man (he points at the Roo who plays both Pyramus and Thisbe in the play-within-the-play and is now dressed in a workman's blue coat) is Pyramus, if you would. This beauteous lady (Quince points at the Roo's other head) Thisbe is certain.

"This man with lime and roughcast doth present," (and Quince points to good friend Stan Hayes who played Wall in the same IWU play so many years ago) 'Wall', that vile wall which did these lovers sunder; And through Wall's chink, poor souls, they are Content to Whisper, at the which let no man wonder."

(Quince points to Mo who plays 'Moonshine'.)

"This man, with lantern, dog and bush of thorn, Presenteth 'Moonshine', for if you will know, By moonshine did these lovers think no scorn; To meet at Ninus' tomb, there to woo.

"This grisly beast, which 'Lion' hight by name," (Quince points at Beth who plays the Lion but is dressed as a DRAGON), "The trusty Thisbe coming first by night, Did scare away or rather did affright; and, as she fled, her mantle she did fall, Which Lion vile with bloody mouth did stain."

And with that last line, a woman in seat 36B did faint! Sean looked up from his double-Kangaroo head, and beheld sweet Grace fallen into a trance as honey-bees danced to wake her up. Grace, finished with her first day of Fish School, had been borne back to the island on the white-faced Dolphin's back. Now home, a little late for her celebration, she had found her fine seat just after the curtain went up. But now on the ground, overcome with lost love emotion, she lay flat on her back while on stage Sean did nothing but pace. Finally making up his mind, he raced down the steps into the audience and toward Grace in his royal costume as, above them, the play continued.

Flute: Oh, Wall, full often hast though heard my moans. For parting my fair Pyramus and me. My cherry lips often kissed they stones, Thy stones with lime and hair knit up in thee."

(Flute kissed the Wall. But STAN HAYES spat in Flute's face, who faints as Grace, by the Grace of God, wakes to find Sean, still disguised as the Two-Headed Roo, waving a thick paper Stage Play Programme in her face.)

The LION, still played by Beth, trounced in onstage in a black Hamlet costume, breathing great tongues of fire!

"Oops, wrong play," said Beth, glancing down at the costume. "I read the prompter incorrectly. I'm costumed inappropriately for the play *Macbeth*, directed by our own Illinois Wesleyan Director Dr John Ficca; or is it a play created by our own play-within-a-play playwright, or is he a novelist, the famous Mr Robert Burda?"

Tearing off her Hamlet costume, Beth donned the costume of the Lion which a stagehand threw to her from offstage and began to ROAR!

Lion: "You ladies, you whose gentle hearts do fear, The smallest monstrous mouse that creeps on floor, May now perchance both quake and tremble here, When lion rough in wildest rage doth roar!"

Mo, playing Moonshine, looked askance.

Moonshine: "This lanthorn doth the horned moon present (Mo holds out an ancient lantern all aglow with fireflies inside, all hotly present). "Myself the man I' th' moon do seem to be. All that I have to say is to tell you that the lanthorn is the moon, I the man I' th' moon, this my thornbush, and this dog my dog (Mo holds up a cardboard cutout of a dog. The Canines in the audience take offense and begin to BARK – BOW-WOW-WOW!!!)

Bottom (acting again as director and also the character Bottom from the play-within-the-play): "Sweet Moon, I thank thee for thy sunny beams ('Mo, why is the lanthorn out!' Bottom yelps. 'Wake up those fireflies before I break my branch of thorn over your fat head!!!')

Beth snickered as Mo worked to defend himself. Stan Hayes chuckled and gets out of the way as Bottom bounced the branch of thorns off of Mo's thick head.

Moonshine: "Oh dainty duck! O dear! O Fates, come, come, cut the thread and thrum, quail, conclude and quell!"

The actors all fell over as, with the rising of the Sun, they concluded the play-within-a-play with a Celebration of Fireworks above the open-air theatre on this, the end of Grace's first full day of Fish School!

The Puck walked back on stage and bowing, said the immortal lines made famous by William Shakespeare:

> "If we shadows have offended,
> Think but this, and all is mended,
> That you have but slumbered here

While these visions did appear.

And this weak and idle theme,

No more yielding but a dream,

Gentles, do not reprehend:

If you pardon, we will mend:

And, as I am an honest Puck,

If we have unearned luck

Now to 'scape the serpent's tongue,

We will make amends ere long;

Else the Puck a liar call;

So, good night unto you all.

Give me your hands, if we be friends,

And Robin shall restore amends."

As the sunlight struck the stage, all of the cast members bowed to the audience. In turn, the audience broke into Great APPLAUSE (and dear Reader, now is the time for you to Applaud, too! So put your hand together not for the cast members, but for William Shakespeare and his incredible work, *A Midsummer Night's Dream*. The words sometimes get in the way of a play-within-a-play when it's written not acted, but it is so, so hysterical when acted on the stage! Be sure to see it anywhere it's played. It's magical and wonderful, and quite funny – a real sight to behold!)

As fireworks go off high overhead, a single golden spotlight of light makes its way across the audience, settling at last on Sean still disguised as the Two-Headed Roo standing over his Juliet, Grace, while she recovers from her faint.

"Oh, Grace, this is not me, the Two-Headed Roo. Nor am I the Monstrous Spider that spun you in my silver web. Look, it is I, your one true shining knight, your Romeo playing to his Juliet."

When Grace glances up, she recognises something that she remembers in the Roo and even the Monstrous Spider's soft eyes, and says, "Is that you Sean? Have you been there all the time?"

With that, Sean transforms from the Roo into the young human being, now dressed in his suit as the Catholic boy who sought to minister, who is also her lost lover.

"Yes, Grace, it is really me who now has the courage to take you up high, and sweep you off your feet with a proposal of marriage. All I have to do is find the ring I gave you, together with my note, that I originally offered to you in Swahili-land but is now buried here to keep both of them close to my heart. But I've forgotten where because my mind is all a-flutter." Sean steps closer to his lost lover. "Help me find them, my sweet Grace. I can't remember because I'm also a Lost Lover, and my head is full of love for you."

Grace, who by now had recovered both from her faint and the knowledge that the Roo and the Spider were all Sean and the same, stared up at him, her heart beating faster.

"You mean you found the diamond engagement ring and the letter you offered to me back at our home in Swahili-land when you first proposed to me?"

Sean nodded. "Don't you remember, I tried to give it to you again in Calcutta? Your mother helped me find it before I journeyed to find you. It was buried right outside the door to your Swahili hut. When you left with so much anger in your heart against me, I had forgotten where I had hid it. But when your mother helped me find it, I took it with me to India. There, I found you working as a jam-boy to make money for the poor and to make ends meet. Don't you remember how I proposed to you in India, too?"

But Grace only shook her head. She had been too injured back then to remember the loving incident.

"I'm still ashamed of what I'd become," Grace said, her eyes falling to her feet. "Why would you ever want to marry a jam-boy? I would rather have starved than have been reduced to that role. I've sinned against everyone, especially you."

At that TRUMPETS BLARED as the last Firework was extinguished and Sean and Grace looked at Bottom who was again on stage.

"Hear ye! Hear ye! All of you animals on land and the ones in the sea, now hear this urgent message from the likes of me," Bottom again cried through fat lips on his conch shell. "This chapter is ended, because the play *Lost Lovers* is finished. And now to end our fable of love lost and found again, we must search the beach from stem to stern to find the lost diamond engagement ring and the note Sean had written to Grace."

Bottom pointed down at the two lost lovers, their arms wrapped around each other.

"So come now, all of you, and join us first in a breakfast feast! Then we'll stomp across the island to look for the ring, and that will be almost the end of our fable. But first, let's eat!"

And the honey-bees buzzed once again. "Why it's Breakfast Time in Magic Land. We love our food, and so do you. Why it's Breakfast Time in our Magic Land! So come with us why don't you… and when we're all full we'll search for a diamond engagement ring."

And with that, we move on to Chapter Fourteen!

Chapter Fifteen

And now let us wind up our story of love that has been lost and found again with a lesson of forgiveness that is given only when people stop arguing with themselves and learn to forget their sins.

As Sean and Grace dashed around the great beach, now flashing gold in the sweet sunshine, they were followed by honeybees and the mechanicals, and other animals too, including fishes and giraffes, koala bears and other great beasts, all intent on finding Sean's diamond ring and the message he'd written so long ago. Grace had told him that she had found the box with the note, but not the diamond engagement ring. But now, having forgotten where it was buried, she scurried across the beach with Sean and deep into the forest, looking for the treasure that would at last wed the two together.

When Sean finally stumbled upon a branch of a gigantic palm tree, he bent his head to see what he had fallen on and thought he laid on a hive of buzzing bumble bees. But when he rose in surprise, he gasped because as he moved a great rock, he found a great hole. And within the hole was a box and when he got down on his knees, he looked up to find Grace standing above him, disappointment lining her graceful sweet face.

"Sean, as I told you, the note is in there but not the diamond engagement ring," she said, looking glumly at him. "I know it's lost forever and ever." Then tears fell on her dark cheeks, and guilt filled her face, because she guessed what Sean wanted to do. You see, her long lost lover was still on two knees with a look of eternal love in his eyes. "Are you going to propose to me again? How can you do that when you know I'm filled with sin?" Grace asked Sean who continued to kneel in the sand. "How can you propose again to a woman like me, who worked as a jam-boy in India to make ends meet?"

But Sean stared hard at her and lifted the lid to the box. There he beheld the note that he'd written for Grace back in her home of Swahili-land. He handed her the letter stained with time and her recent tears and, as the animals watched, Grace cleared her throat and this time read out-loud what Sean had written so long ago and which she had read only once the day before:

"My dearest Grace. I'll love you forever, no matter where you may go or what you may do. Our love is eternal, forever and ever, and forevermore. And one day, I promise I'll find you because I'll always love you no matter what you do."

Sean looked up at her. "Grace, don't you hear the words you speak? I don't care what you did before. That's all water under the bridge. I don't even need the note to remember what I wrote all those years ago." He rose, taking her in his arms and repeated his words from memory. "*'And one day, I promise I'll find you because I'll always love you no matter what you do.'* Which means, my eternal love, I've always forgiven you but there's no need for forgiveness because none of it was your fault. Now can't you forgive *yourself* for what you were forced to do years ago in India, and let me just love you?"

With that, Grace looked out over the horizon at the glittering ocean thinking that a choir of Angels had begun to sing. At sea, escorted toward the island by a throng of dolphins, with the White-faced Dolphin leading the pod, the Long-Lost Ghost of Mother Teresa of India walked toward Grace on the water.

When the Saint was escorted by the dolphins to the safety of the beach, she took Grace's hand in her wrinkled strong fingers, and studied her face with a solemn look that lingered.

"Oh Grace, can't you see that I forgave you so many years ago. But there was nothing to forgive because you worked as a jam-boy so you could give to the poor, just as your long-lost-love Sean did before? Forgive yourself now, and by all the saints in Heaven, I bless Sean's proposal with a loving proclamation."

Grace knelt down by Sean upon the glowing beach as leopards and tigers and elephants also knelt, as did the fishes of the sea. As her dark eyes cast down on the sand, Grace dared not to look up at the Holy Saint Teresa.

"Forgive me, Mother, for what I have done…"

"Stop it, Grace, your guilt is so unnecessary, so look upon me and know you are already forgiven the day you were born!"

Then the Saint of India raised her right hand and made the Sign of the Cross, blessing all who had gathered around in the sand.

"Bless this great Zoo which our Father has made," Saint Teresa continued. "Blessed be the animals of all races and sexual preferences, the tigers and bears, the lions and humans. Bless and forgive them, dear Father in Heaven, that Grace may understand that forgiveness is a miracle which has not been lost forever, but is here for the asking and taking if she and we all want it. Now rise, fair Grace, you are the Queen of this Earth and your village of Jua, so come now to me and claim your Global heaven."

With that, another miracle happened. As Grace rose, taking Sean's hand, a choir of Saints sang from the trees, and a circus of apes blew conch shells made of angel wings. Then from Grace's head sprang a halo so mighty, it sang on its own for it was made by God the Almighty. Upon Grace's brow, light cast its great circle that Saints and Angels wear when Bishops and Cardinals and even Popes kneel before them.

Then Grace looked up as Sean looked back into the box and another miracle occurred, given by God and Holy Saint Teresa. Sean beheld a fair diamond ring sparkling in the sunlight, the one he'd bought Grace years before when he was only a simple missionary attempting to teach the *Lord's Prayer* and *Hail Mary* to the gifted Swahili kids.

"Oh Grace, my fair Maid, look what God and Saint Teresa of Calcutta has thought to bring?" he said, finding the ring. Picking it up, he held it out to his future bride, then put it on her finger and it glittered in the sun as though it might sing. "Will you marry me, I ask, for the third time in my life? Will you be mine forever, as my one true, eternal wife?"

With that, the dolphins and fishes and animals all sang in a chorus, as Grace looked at the ring with eyes that were enormous.

"Oh Sean, my fair Romeo, your Juliet says yes. It's the dawn of a new life, with a new chapter before us."

***

And so our Play and Story *Lost Lovers* ends, as the huge passenger ship, the Queen Elizabeth, having sailed into the harbour to collect the happy couple, once again embarked on a voyage from the Magical Island back to the fabled land of America.

Once back to the New Continent of milk and honey and paved golden streets and, having completed its journey and with its deck crowded with passengers, they cried with joy as they saw the Statue of Liberty holding her torch of freedom high. And on the day of their arrival, on Fourth of July, the Queen Elizabeth brought not only the world's tired and poor, but two married people who were now expecting their first-born little girl.

As the ship rounded Staten Island, a choir of US Marine's broke into chorus, singing *The Star Spangled Banner*. Then the author of this novel, Tom Richards, repeated the lines of Abe Lincoln's speech of liberty and death; a speech that many thought would bring the end of slavery and suffering to America, a land of honey but also sin. When Richards stepped up to the podium from within a large crowd gathered on the New York pier to welcome the Queen Elizabeth and our happy couple, Sean and Grace, he said solemnly into a microphone:

"Ladies and Gentlemen throughout this Great Land, I speak a speech given by our beloved President, Abraham Lincoln."

Then he cleared his throat and began to speak just as the Young Lincoln did following a great Civil War, a speech that was the beginning of peace:

"Four score and seven years ago our fathers brought forth on this continent a new nation, conceived in Liberty, and dedicated to the proposition that all men are created equal.

"Now we are engaged in a great civil war, testing whether that nation, or any nation so conceived and so dedicated, can long endure. We are met on a great battle-field of that war. We have come to dedicate a portion of that field, as a final resting place for those who here gave their lives that that nation might live. It is altogether fitting and proper that we should do this.

"But, in a larger sense, we can not dedicate—we can not consecrate—we can not hallow—this ground. The brave men, living and dead, who struggled here, have consecrated it, far above our poor power to add or detract. The world will little note, nor long remember what we say here, but it can never forget what they did here. It is for us the living, rather, to be dedicated here to the unfinished work which they who

fought here have thus far so nobly advanced. It is rather for us to be here dedicated to the great task remaining before us—that from these honored dead we take increased devotion to that cause for which they gave the last full measure of devotion—that we here highly resolve that these dead shall not have died in vain— that this nation, under God, shall have a new birth of freedom—and that government of the people, by the people, for the people, shall not perish from the earth."

Finished with the speech, Richards looked up from the podium as Grace and Sean embarked from the Queen Elizabeth, just as fireworks danced in the skies far above them.

"I am proud to express the words of Abraham Lincoln in his young voice," the writer said shyly. "They should have asked the Bard of many films, famous actor Gregory Peck, to say the President's hallowed words because that actor's voice has the gravity necessary for this amazing occasion."

Abe Lincoln's Gettysburg Address as portrayed by Tom Richards available here

***

And so it's time for a final Coda by me, your narrator, Kylie Whipple.

As it turned out, Sean and Grace moved to the land of milk and honey for the rest of their lives and raised many good children who still help to populate America and many other foreign lands because many of the characters in this story, as you know Dear Reader, aren't fiction but as real as you. And yes, that's the end of our play but only the beginning of yours.

Remember to keep praying for help and, like the Lady in Heaven told me before, as did Saint Teresa of Calcutta and Saint Brigid of Ireland, we can't pray for ourselves but rather each other. You see, these blessed people whispered to me one night, into an ear filled with wax so filled up it wasn't right, that the *Our Father* is all about ourselves and our families, not only our Savior. So too is every *Hail Mary* you pray all about how you and your loved ones will eventually go to Heaven, come what may. And no matter what you pray, or whatever your religion, or even if you don't have a religion but are an atheist, it matters not because it's never selfish to ask for help, as long as you live by the Golden Rule and treat everyone just like you. Like Grace and Sean, we can only try our hardest to get through each day. And if you still need help, you might think to reach out to Saint Teresa of Calcutta, and also to Saint Brigid, the Patron Saint of Ireland, who are always there for you.

Be well, dear Reader, and remember to forgive yourself and each other…because that's really all we have to do.

And that's finally the end of our tale, and all this narrator has left to say about that, quoting, in the final lines, from the film *Forrest Gump….*

LIFE IS LIKE A BOX OF CHOCOLATES

Sometimes sweet, sometimes bitter. But always, always different and surprising to every taste and reader.

The End

<u>Acknowledgements</u>

Before moving onto the people who must be mentioned, may I refer to Puck's Shakespearean quote at the end of the play-within-a-play:

"If we shadows have offended, think but this and all is mended…give me your hands, if we be friends, and Robin shall restore amends."

While all the characters in *A Midsummer Night's Dream* are fiction, Shakespeare made them real to us. Like this play-within-a-play, much of what you've read is based on real life stories, just as Shakespeare wrote in his Tragedies, Comedies, and Histories.

So first, a big call-out to a guy a met who's become a fast friend. If it hadn't been for Johnny Morrisey, this volume would never have been written. Jam-boys are critically important to this novel and were real people (for all I know, they still are). Both girls and boys, their naked bodies were smeared with jam and honey. They were made to run across golf courses naked, attracting flies and honey bees so that their Lords and Masters, both Indian and English, would not be bothered by any insects as they played their games of golf. Then, after that, these so-called gentlemen raped and pillaged these naked warriors. So it was in Old English India. As I say, Jam-Boys are vital to this story of Lost Love and Bitter Memories. Most of us have both – true love followed by a broken heart. Because of Johnny, who met me in a local pub and mentioned the term 'jam boy' (which I'd never heard of before but after which I did extensive research) I realized it that abuse was a central theme of this novel. And so, Grace encounters both Heartbreak and Happiness during her stay in India.

Mother Teresa is also very real. Google her and you'll find that she really is a Catholic Saint. Grace is based on many women I've known: the poor and rich, the homeless and wealthy. She truly is based on many human beings I've known and now, to me, she seems more than real.

Many of the other characters in this novella are also based on true-to-life people. Friends and relatives of mine. Colleagues and distant cousins. Though they do not know which characters are based on them, these are all saints too, just like my Aunt Wini. Christians, Evangelicals, LBGQ, Muslims, Arabians, Jews, Hindus – people from every persuasion of life – are combined to make up many of the characters in this story.

Once again, may I remind you, Dear Reader, of what Puck says above: *"If we shadows but offend, think but this and all is mended…"* So, if I've offended, please reach out and accept my hand in friendship.

As I write above, if this writer has offended anyone, please accept my apologies. The world, as Kylie states in the story, is full of happiness but we also have their fare share of heartbreak.

Now this writer turns to the rest of this short ending of the novella, *Lost Lovers*:

In addition to the people mentioned in the Dedication Page, this author would like to call out the invaluable contribution William Shakespeare has made to English literature. If it was not for this Bard of playwriting and sonnets, few would ever start writing.

To reader and Storylines Entertainment Ltd colleague and fellow writer Claire O'Connor, thank you for your constant help. To Barbara Klaw, professional editor, I thank you for your many comments and advice. You spotted the inherent confusion this novelist tried to write. And Barb, no this is not an autobiography. It's fiction based somewhat on fact. I think it is anyway. See? Even this writer gets confused sometimes as to what genre this is written in.

To my great High School buddy, Will Arnold (he also goes by the name of Wil Rogers, the famous songster cowboy, who always rode on a white horse). A sometimes poet, and very occasionally superb, he loves making fun of this author as you can see by his reader comment, well above.

To the doctors and nurses at Bantry General Hospital and Cork University Hospital, particularly Nurse Teresa, thank you for your constant care as I continue to recover from my recent Heart Attack (P.S. I'm feeling GREAT!)

May I mention Toqueer (who was responsible for the cover and formatting) and Grammargirl (my wonderful editor) both of whom you can contact by referring to the Copyright page and their individual URLs. Both are talented and gifted and I *always* strongly recommend them on their fiverr pages. May I also thank Divya and her team who contributed so much to this novel through their inspiring illustrations.

To my dear friends Ron Raben, Steve Courtney, and Robert Burda – all have passed on to, as Grace says in the novel, "A heaven of milk and honey". I miss you all.

And finally, to Carmel Murray, forever my loving inspiration: Carm now suffers from Early Onset Alzheimer's disease, though she is only 59 years old as I type. As those of you who understand such an illness know, it makes sufferers behave like children. While this short novel is not dedicated to her, know that my heart is always focused on her: to her wants and needs and a future of happiness – not heartbreak – and a future that I know will one day include our marriage. Alzheimer's patients can get married, you know, even if they forget each other – just as Sean and Grace do at the end of the story. It's not about poetry or narrative: it's about two hearts that are twined together: just like Carm's and Tom's, these are two people meant to live their lives together, forever.

I miss my Carm and will do anything for you.

Tom Richards
Eyeries, Beara, Bantry, County Cork, Ireland, P75 A342
www.tomrichards.ie   tomrichards141@gmail.com
July, 2022